HONORS DUE

Books *by* EDWARD CLINE

Chess Hanrahan Novels

Honors Due (2011)
Presence of Mind (2010)
First Prize (2010)

Sparrowhawk Novels

Sparrowhawk Book Six: War (2006)
Sparrowhawk Book Five: Revolution (2005)
Sparrowhawk Book Four: Empire (2004)
Sparrowhawk Book Three: Caxton (2004)
Sparrowhawk Book Two: Hugh Kenrick (2002)
Sparrowhawk Book One: Jack Frake (2001)

Other Novels

We Three Kings (2010)
Whisper the Guns (1992)

Nonfiction

The Sparrowhawk Companion (2007)

HONORS DUE

A Chess Hanrahan Novel

EDWARD CLINE

PERFECT CRIME BOOKS

Library of Congress Cataloging-in-Publication Data
Cline, Edward
Honors Due / Edward Cline
ISBN: 978-1-935797-14-2

First Edition: June 2011

There may be cities who refuse
To their own child the honours due,
And look ungently on the Muse;
But ever shall those cities rue
The dry, unyielding, niggard breast,
Offering no nourishment, no rest,
To that young head which soon shall rise
Disdainfully, in might and glory, to the skies.

Walter Savage Landor

Chapter 1

"I found your son, Mrs. Sismond," I said to the arrogant, expectant face, "but I'm afraid I can't tell you where he is."

"What do you mean?" she asked, her voice hovering between outrage and astonishment.

"Harry doesn't want to be a philanthropist."

Mrs. George L. Sismond—Beatrice to her friends, of which she might have had a few—blinked once at me and sat for a moment weighing whether or not she would allow herself to absorb the meaning of my words. After all, I'd flown here all the way from New York to tell her this, when I could have just as easily told her over the phone. It was my presence her mind was stumbling over. Her big, doubled-paned, soundproof living room windows overlooked San Francisco Bay and a gorgeous view of the Golden Gate Bridge. I contemplated the towers beyond her thin face and waited for her to respond.

The Sismonds of San Francisco were very wealthy. George L. Sismond, five years deceased, had made millions long ago in

Pacific shipping, then retired to live long enough to establish, apparently at his wife's behest, the George L. Sismond Foundation for Social Concerns and Problems. His wife succeeded him as chairman of its board of directors.

Two weeks ago, in New York, the day after Columbus Day, she'd called my office and invited me to her suite at the Plaza Hotel to discuss the problem of her missing younger son, Harry, recently graduated from Stanford. She'd come to the city to see friends, to catch some of the fall social whirl, and to attend *La Traviata*, *Aida*, and Clovis Pillataire's reputedly sensational operatic rendering of Proust's *Jean Santeuil* at the Met. Before talking business she marveled at the city and asked me about my background. When she learned that I occasionally attended opera, she asked my opinion of the Met productions. I said I'd seen *La Traviata* and it was all right, I hadn't seen this season's *Aida*, and I didn't plan to see *Jean Santeuil*.

"Why not, Mr. Hanrahan?" she'd asked. "Are you against the *new*?"

"No," I said. "The opera critic on the *Times* panned it."

"So you heed critics."

"Not usually." In this case, the reviewer had compared the score to an orchestra's warm-up cacophony, measured the libretto against track announcements in Grand Central, and summed up the story as "bits and pieces that got stuffed into Swann's dive." Esthetic honesty is rare these days, and when I encounter it, I heed it. I didn't tell Mrs. Sismond any of that.

"Well, to each his own," she said, color coming to her face. I thought then that she was upset because she probably had box seats to *Jean Santeuil*. I learned the actual reason later.

She had picked me as an investigator because I was something of a celebrity in New York. She read the West Coast edition of the Manhattan *Times*, which sometimes ran stories about my cases. Some of her friends had recommended me. "I'm told that you can be a perfect stinker, Mr. Hanrahan," she said, "but that you get things done. I hope you don't mind my being so frank with you."

"Not at all," I'd said, "if you won't mind my being frank with you, if and when the need arises."

Mrs. Sismond answered with that classic, insincere smile that meant, "Of course not," but which was a warning not to be frank with her. "You must be curious why I've hired you and not someone of your profession in San Francisco."

I'd shrugged. "San Francisco is a smaller town. You probably won't want to risk it becoming common knowledge that your son is missing."

"That's correct," she said. She explained the goals of her foundation and how a possibly scandalous incident might damage its reputation. I was familiar with the Sismond Foundation for Social Concerns and Problems. It was wealthy and loopy, famous for donating money in equal sums to antithetical causes. It had subsidized the legal expenses of opposing parties in libel suits, in class action suits, and in discrimination suits against private clubs. It contributed to classical ballet and to avant-garde dance, to realist and abstract schools of art, to traveling folk art collections, to classical music academies and folk music festivals. It donated to public television stations, and it supported efforts to house hobos and reeducate juvenile delinquents.

A special program, she told me, made lifetime grants to writers and artists of "proven talent." "Three of the current best-selling novelists are Sismond Life Fellows, Mr. Hanrahan, as are four prominent painters, two sculptors, three solo musicians, and one operatic composer." She'd paused to let the significance of the last sink in, then said, "It was my late husband's opinion that we should merely provide gloves for the opponents, and to let society determine what is best for everyone. I endorse that sentiment one hundred percent. That sentiment, of course, refers to all our non-cultural endeavors, as well."

I smiled my own plastic smile. "How does your son Harry feel?"

Mrs. Sismond frowned, dismissing the question with a wave of her hand. "Harry? Harry's always agreed with me, but he's also a bit wild. Not completely unpredictable, mind you, but wild enough to take me by surprise at times. This is one of those times. He's utterly without ambition, and he resisted being absorbed into the Foundation's work. I've never understood that. He's the absolute opposite of my older son, Charles. Charles took a degree in social policy at Harvard and brought many new ideas to the Foundation. But Harry—well, my position is that, since he is without a scrap of purpose, there is no good reason why he can't continue in his father's and brother's footsteps." She paused. "If I could just talk to him, I know I could persuade him to stop this foolishness and come back. He can't do anything else, really. He couldn't sustain himself out there, in the workaday world. He's never lacked for anything and wouldn't know otherwise how to get it. God only knows what kinds of people he'd meet and who might take advantage of him. He was supposed to have reported to the Foundation a month ago, as we'd all understood he would."

She knew only that he hadn't left the country. His passport was still in his room, and conversations with some of his friends at Stanford led her to believe that they were hiding the truth of his whereabouts. He'd confided in no one associated with his family. Some clothes and two of his bankbooks and credit cards were missing. He'd left a note that read: "Dear Mom: I've got to think things over. Please don't try to find me. I'll call. Harry." Mrs. Sismond had found it a day after he was to have reported for work at the Foundation. The Missing Persons Bureau had had no luck in tracing him.

So I had Mrs. Sismond sign a standard contract, write me a retainer check, and give me a photograph of her son and a list of his friends. I flew out to San Francisco that night. I followed a bizarre trail that included a couple of Stanford professors, classmates, girlfriends, fraternity friends, his last apartment manager in Palo Alto, and restaurant and café managers. I had little time to sightsee, worked out of an airport motel room, and developed a distaste for the job. Looking for an answer was like doing an acrostic puzzle letter by agonizing letter, only to find at the end that the sentence was something in Serbian.

But I found Harry Sismond, back in New York, working as an apprentice ozalid machine operator for a printing company that did blueprints for construction firms. The company was owned by the father of one of his former classmates. Harry truly hadn't wanted to be found, for a very different reason than either his mother or I could have imagined.

"Would you mind explaining why you can't tell me where my son is?" Mrs. Sismond asked, interrupting my appreciation of the Bridge.

"He doesn't want you to know where he is," I said. "He wants to be out of your reach for a while. That may mean months or years. He doesn't know yet. But he was quite emphatic about it."

"He told *you* that he doesn't want to work for the Foundation?"

"In many more words, but not exactly. Going by what he did say, it was a pretty easy conclusion to reach."

Mrs. Sismond shot up out of her leather armchair and glared at me. "Your conclusions don't concern me, Mr. Hanrahan! I hired you to locate my son and then to notify me of his whereabouts, and that's all!"

I permitted myself a smile. "I think he's right."

"You . . . you're taking *his* side?"

"I don't like your son, Mrs. Sismond. There are a few things wrong with him, and certain aspects of his character don't endear him to me. But maybe a little time in the real world — the working world, not the Foundation world — will straighten him out. He knows he needs straightening out. Give him credit, and a chance."

"Where is he, goddamn you?"

"I won't tell you," I said. I rose, reached inside my jacket, and took out two envelopes. "That's why I'm returning your retainer check and waiving all the expenses I've incurred. Your son paid for my ticket out here and back to New York." I put the envelope with the check on the stand beside my chair.

Mrs. Sismond's eyes widened, and she gasped. "This is *preposterous!*"

I shook my head. "No, not at all, Mrs. Sismond. It's apparent that the people who recommended me to you have an odd notion of what a stinker is." I paused. "Your son isn't a fur wrap or a season ticket to the opera you've lost and want returned to you. He's a living being who walks and talks and thinks after a fashion. He wants to know something about the real world, or at least what else there might be besides fur wraps and season tickets and spending a father's fortune. That's the behavior of a man in search of a purpose."

Mrs. Sismond opened her mouth to reply, but I took a step forward and held out the second envelope. "Harry paid for my air fare so I could give you this. It's a personal note from him. A kind of postscript to his first note."

Mrs. Sismond didn't see the envelope. "He could have mailed it and saved you the discomfort of being told in person that I'm going to sue you for breach of contract!"

I stared her down and added, "He asked me to deliver this to you personally, and wait for a reply. If you have one."

She snatched the envelope from my hand and turned angrily to rip it open. With her back to me she read the single handwritten page. After a while she turned in another direction, away from me, her hands aimless and fluttery. I could see her eyes were watery with repressed emotion. She said, "I . . . I have no reply . . . not yet. I'll contact you when I do. Now, I think you'd better go, Mr. Hanrahan."

I collected my coat from a chair in an anteroom and left. In the penthouse foyer I pressed an elevator button, then stood at the picture window as I waited and admired the Golden Gate Bridge without distraction. I wondered how many thousands of tons of shipping her husband had brought in from the Far East under its span. It must have been new when he started his business decades ago. It wasn't just his fortune that was being squandered, I thought. It was his effort, his success, his reputation. I doubted that the Foundation had been his idea. Anyway, it was over, and I washed my hands of the matter. I would call Harry, brief him on what had happened, and hope that was the last I heard of it.

I emerged from the pink pastel tower on Russian Hill and walked a while. I had a whole day left to myself before taking another night flight back to New York, twelve hours to spend in a city I didn't particularly like.

There was too little time to do much more than have dinner and see a movie. There were museums, and the sights, of course, but I would be rushed and I didn't like being rushed. I'd slept well on the plane, and wasn't so much tired as in a sour mood. I had no hotel to go back to; all I'd brought with me this time was an overnight bag with a change of shirt and things and it was stashed in a locker at the airport. There weren't as many cruising cabs as there were in New York and I was halfway back downtown before I could hail one in front of the Fairmont on Nob Hill. Then I changed my mind, waved it on, and went inside the hotel. In the lobby, I sat with a cigarette and glanced through a magazine, *What's Doing in Town*. In the movie section I noted that one of the theaters was having a Patrick Player festival. Today it was featuring *Drums of the Fore and Aft* and *Falling Bodies*.

Player was once one of my favorite actors. In fact, the whole Player family—Cedric, Malcolm, and Patrick—rated my five stars. *Drums* was the first of Patrick's and the last of grandfather Cedric's pictures, based on a Rudyard Kipling story. I'd first seen it when I was eight years old, and I cried at the end when Lew and Jakin, the British army band boys, were cut down by Afghan bullets just as they'd succeeded in rallying their regiment with their fife and drum. It was the first grand-scale picture I'd ever seen, in the loge of a big-screen palace in Manhattan. My father had taken me. I smiled in memory of the afternoon. I was still undecided about which I owed a greater debt to: the picture itself, by which I'd unconsciously begun to measure all subsequent movies; or my father, who had put a hand on my shoulder, but hadn't laughed, and hadn't told me it was only a story.

Falling Bodies, though, was released some five years ago, and I had never seen it. I'd stopped following Patrick Player's career after he began appearing in ecological horror pictures and had starred in half a dozen box office bombs. Going by what the critics had written with approval about the flicks, I hadn't bothered to see any of them. His name also appeared frequently in the Manhattan *Times* theater page listings. But it wasn't the same Patrick Player I'd known.

So, after a lunch in the hotel restaurant, I went back outside, hailed a cab, and went to the movies.

Chapter 2

People today were so inured to modern movie credits—which were often so complex and belabored that they required their own director and crew—that few audiences paid them much attention. But if a picture was polished from beginning to end, then the opening credits could serve as a prelude. *Falling Bodies*, which I'd arrived just in time to catch, had that touch, and it surprised me. It had been made only five years ago. Its credits gave me a thrill I usually felt only for pictures made decades ago.

They appeared in gold script on a dark velvet background, and were accompanied by Respighi's "Ancient Aires and Dances." The sight and sound silenced the audience around me. Murmured conversations died quickly and cellophane candy wrappings stopped crackling.

So, with the rest of the audience, I sat back and watched the story unfold. It concerned Galileo's trial by the Church for endorsing the Copernican system of the solar system. It starred Patrick Player as Galileo, Dean Tolland as Cardinal Bellarmine, and Kimberly Eames, probably the most exquisite, enchanting actress to come out of Hollywood in twenty years. The supporting cast was perfect, with Kit Aragon, Allan Swain, and other actors I respected, Lately I'd seen them less often in pictures of stature and more in stereotyped roles in soap operas.

And, with the audience, I was slapped in the face. The picture was a farce. Not a straight farce, but great drama alternating with slapstick, risqué comedy. It built up characters, then tore then down. Only the comedians remain untouched.

I glanced at some of the faces around me. I saw pain, fear and hope—I would have bet it was a hope that what was happening up on the screen wasn't actually happening.

But it was. I stood up and walked out of the theater less than halfway through the picture. I sat in the lobby and had a cigarette. I felt abused. It was as though someone had wrenched out my soul and spray-painted it with dirty pictures. I wavered between blaming myself for having expected more, and blaming Player and the director and the cast for having suckered me. I settled for blaming Player and company.

Galileo. On one hand a man of integrity and incredible courage. On the other, a two-timing, lecherous buffoon inveigling his way into a Cardinal's favor—according to Patrick Player, according to George Soquel, the director, according to Leonard Sproul and Albert Grunnian, producers. Before this afternoon, Player had simply bored me. I'd buried my disappointment with his later career. Now I think I actually hated him, because he could have redeemed himself in *Falling Bodies* and created a great picture.

Kimberly Eames, I reflected. So beautiful and talented that she'd made the covers of most national news magazines long before she appeared in her first picture. She radiated sensual innocence even when she looked bored. She could be toweringly formidable when she was supposed to be frightened. My favorite image of her was the look of worship she could give a man; it was something a man could worship, too, if he had sense enough to understand it. In the picture, the director had used her as a tease. I'd stopped following her career, too. I wasn't certain that she'd appeared in anything after *Falling Bodies*. She had dropped out of sight and out of the realm of my concerns.

I left the theater, hailed another cab, and spent the rest of the day on a walking tour of downtown. I tried the bookstores and art galleries, then had dinner in another hotel restaurant that overlooked Union Square. If the city had any charms, they were lost on me. Both Mrs. Sismond and *Falling Bodies* had left me in a surly mood. I wound up buying a copy of Henry Sumner Maine's *Popular Government* in a second-hand store and sitting in a coffee shop with it until it was time to take a cab to the airport.

And on the plane I skipped the snack and had a quart of coffee as I tried to finish the third essay. I was still in a venomous temper and couldn't concentrate. Something was bothering me, and I couldn't pin it down.

Harry Sismond. Once I'd found him, I invited him to lunch in a deli up the street from his job in the SoHo district. He was the reason I'd taken the case, and I wanted to size him up and see whether he'd been worth it. He was a lost lamb—a brave lamb— but lost nonetheless, a nice looking kid of twenty-one with pliant features that might someday harden into character. When I met him he looked a bit exhausted. The working world had shaken him. The hardest part for him was not the work, which he found fascinating—"Did you know they even make blueprints for things like screws and clamps and staples and stuff like that?" — but having to deal with his bosses and coworkers. They were nothing like he'd ever encountered before in his brief, insular life. They left him baffled. How could he deal with them?

"Patronize the best in them and keep an arm's length from their worst," I suggested.

"What's their best and worst?"

"That's for you to decide."

"Well, how do you know?"

Now I was baffled. "Whatever makes you like them, or whatever makes you indifferent, or disgusted."

"That's hard to tell, what's likeable or disgusting. Maybe you and I wouldn't like or hate the same things in people."

"What made you leave home?" I asked. "If you'd stayed and taken up your mother's Foundation work, you wouldn't need to bother with such problems."

Harry lowered his head and stared into his chilled coffee. "I left home because I got *tired* of . . . people always arranging my life for me. Everywhere I turned, people were doing things for me, or wanting to do them, fixing this and fixing that, clearing the way for me. Me, the golden boy, the heir to the fabulous Sismond pile or at least a big hunk of it. Everyone did it, the profs, the guys in the fraternity. It reached a point when I began to feel *I* didn't exist! I was coasting through like a ghost. I didn't have to do anything. The only effort I had to make was to keep a grade point average. But you don't go through life just to maintain grade point averages, do you? And whatever little they let me do for myself, like actually work for a grade instead of some sly prof passing me anyway, well, it was only to tie me to them somehow. To something . . . corrupt."

I lit a cigarette, offered him one from the nickel case and lit it for him. Harry Sismond paused, coughed. "For a long while, I knew what was going on, and why, and didn't mind it. But the closer graduation came, the scareder I got. I knew what was waiting for me up in the city at the Foundation. Just Mom and Charles and the executives and the office they had all ready for me. I'd have had a great view of the Bay. But, you see, I had this weird idea—sometimes I even had nightmares about it—that if anyone looked from one of the other towers into my office, they wouldn't see anyone. Do you understand any of that?"

I nodded. "You've taken yourself seriously. And you've seen that it's more than most people do. It's a first step."

"What's the next step?"

"Keep looking."

Harry found that funny, snickered. I didn't like his sense of humor.

"Or you could pack up and go back to Mom and your brother."

He took a final draw on his cigarette and tamped it out in the foil ashtray. "Look, you don't have to tell my mother you found me. Just say you couldn't."

I shook my head. "No. I've a reputation to keep up. And why should I lie on your behalf? That would just be someone clearing the way for you again. Wouldn't it?"

Harry looked solemn for the first time. Solemn and unconsciously proud.

I liked the look. I liked it so much that I said, "I'll tell you what. I'll be your messenger boy. You write your mother a note, telling her in the frankest terms you can think of what you think of her, of her plans for you, and so on. Tell her why you left, the way you told me. I'll deliver it, in person. You pay my round trip fare to San Francisco and back. Don't hide anything or try to butter her up or she'll just think you're kidding. If she hires another detective, he might haul you back for the bounty."

Harry studied me for a moment. "Wouldn't you be breaking your contract with her?"

"Don't worry about it. That's my risk."

"Why are you doing this?"

I grinned. "Why? Maybe I want to protect your freedom to de-brainwash yourself."

So that evening Harry Sismond came up to my office on Thirty-fourth Street and wrote his letter on my stationery. I made a photocopy of it and had him sign a brief statement of his intentions, in case Mrs. Sismond decided she should sue me. I booked a seat on a night flight to San Francisco four hours later. Harry wandered around my office, looked out the window at my south view of Manhattan, and noticed my motto on a brass plaque on the wall near the door:

NOTHING THAT IS OBSERVABLE IN REALITY
IS EXEMPT FROM RATIONAL SCRUTINY.

"Yeah, sure," he scoffed. "You can't really mean that, can you?"

I looked up from sealing his letter in an envelope. "You wouldn't be here if I didn't."

Harry tried to digest my reply. He was still trying to when he left.

So I went out to San Francisco, delivered the message, saw half of a rotten movie, and headed back, feeling sour. Outside the plane window, pools of white and yellow light floated past, patterns that made me sleepy but which wouldn't let me nod off simply because they fascinated me. I asked the stewardess for a couple of aspirin. They only cleared my head and made me uneasier. But I managed to doze off, and woke up to the pilot's announcement that we were beginning the final descent over New York.

Chapter 3

By Friday morning I'd recovered enough from jet lag to get to my office by eight-thirty. I was still in an inexplicably foul mood. I couldn't imagine that it stemmed from the Player picture I'd seen, or from my encounter with Beatrice Sismond. I tried to trace it to something else, but my mind didn't seem to want to work, either.

The morning went by uneventfully. I paid some bills, listened to two messages on my answering machine, neither of which mattered, and answered correspondence that had been collecting on my desk for over a week. And I read. Business was slow. I wasn't looking for it. It usually came to me. I turned a page of Maine's *Popular Government*, and it was then I thought I knew what was bothering me, and I put the book down.

Perhaps all the knowledge I'd acquired over the last four years was making me impatient with people. Intolerably impatient. Shouldn't knowledge and perspective have allowed me to make peace with men and the world, instead of making me tired, hostile, and impatient?

Then I remembered the faces of the people in the audience in that San Francisco theater, faces that strained with what I guessed was hope that what they were seeing wasn't really there, faces so desperate for what had been promised that they would accept it as farce.

The phone rang then and interrupted my thoughts. I picked up the receiver and answered civilly. It was Society calling again, this time in the person of Elaine Card, wife of Edwin Card, Manhattan real estate developer. She wanted to invite me to a banquet, was in the neighborhood, and could she drop up in a few minutes to see me? I said yes. Somewhere in my desk was an RSVP from her that I'd forgotten to answer. It had to do with a charity affair for some cause.

She came half an hour later. She was a nice looking woman, about my age, a younger version of Beatrice Sismond. She was wearing more money than I'd ever made in this office, not counting whatever she carried in her neo-Fifties patent leather purse. By the look on her face, I supposed she had expected a trendier office: pastel blobs on the walls, antiques in an anteroom, a detective in an Italian Deco tie. I was in shirtsleeves, wearing a Tripler's tie, in an office with twice the square footage of a freight elevator. She noticed the print of Raphael's "School of Athens" on one wall and Schreyvogel's "Even Chances" on another. Her glance slid over the motto in brass by the door so slickly that the words couldn't have registered. Her face said: What's a Society man doing in this dump?

She sat in the leather guest chair and after preliminary chitchat asked me to attend a charity dinner at the Waldorf next week— only a thousand dollars a plate—and to sign a petition asking Congress to do something about a number of mental illnesses. My name, she said, would lend great prestige to the cause, along with one hundred fifty-nine other prestigious names. The money raised by the banquet would be donated to various medical research centers experimenting with cures to these illnesses, and in addition maintain her committee's offices down in Washington. At the banquet I might meet some important people and even pick up some business. "Just think of all the scandals you could scare up, Mr. Hanrahan!" she laughed. "If *you* attended, everybody would have to be on their best behavior!"

I said, "That would be pretty dull, wouldn't it?"

"Well, we'll just have to risk it!"

I was feeling hostile again. I sighed. "Mrs. Card, why is it that when you people get together to have fun, it always has to do with charity? Can't you stand each other's company otherwise?"

"Excuse me?"

"If you're going to get together with the tuxes and gowns and jewelry and the open bars and dance bands, why can't you do it just for those reasons?"

"I don't quite understand you, Mr. Hanrahan," said Mrs. Card. "This is to be a public affair. The mayor and several people from the United Nations and even the press will be there. And some actors will do scenes from 'Of Mice and Men.' It's going to be a thrilling and interesting evening."

"The problem is," I said, "I'm not worried about hell."

"What?"

"Your gathering reminds me of an old tradition: people buying indulgences, to gain time in heaven or reduce time in hell. It was trendy in the Middle Ages. I'm not worried about hell, or heaven either now that I think about it, so I'll pass."

Mrs. Card clasped her purse closer to her. "This is for a very good cause, Mr. Hanrahan."

"Made to order, like a dress bought off the rack. You don't buy your dresses off the rack, do you?"

"I'm sure *you've* forgotten to whom you're speaking."

I shook my head. "No, not at all. Elaine Card, cynosure of the social season. At Otherwise Useless College, chair of Delta Sigma Theta, dervish member of the Leaders Council, chairthing of this, secretary of that. Younger and prettier, a volunteer at the kissing booth at spring bust-out. Major in communications, minor in sociology."

Probably none of it was on target, but it was close enough that she departed, with her invitation, leaving behind some rude words she'd probably picked up in a contemporary feminist literature course.

Well, that effectively took care of my standing in this year's Society. I might read about myself in someone's gossip column: *Chess Hanrahan, of the New York Hanrahans, noted* bon vivant *and private detective, declined an invitation to Elaine Card's fabulous feed fest for funny farm fibroma last week, sending Our Lady of Loopiness into a frothy snit.*

I was still feeling nasty enough that I didn't want to deal with anyone else, not even over the phone. So I closed the office early. I glanced through the paper to see what was showing in the museums. The Morgan Library was hosting a "Raphael and His Circle" exhibit. It promised a reprieve from the Mrs. Cards.

It delivered more. I stumbled on what had been bothering me.

The exhibit featured drawings and studies by Michelangelo, Fra Angelico, and a few others. I spent a lot of time in front of Angelico's "Head of a Cleric." It was a sketch, done in the Fifteenth Century, according to the card, in meta point on brown wash, with an ochre preparation. There was intelligence and serenity in the model's mature face. The word "cleric" threw me off until I remembered that in Angelico's time it was also synonymous with "intellectual." The portrait was what I hoped I looked like, and what I felt inside myself. If there was an intellectual who looked like that today, you wouldn't find him at Elaine Card's charity banquets.

Then the image tripped another connection. I remembered a modern face that *did* resemble Fra Angelico's subject. It had appeared on the jacket flap of a number of biographies I'd read over the last year, written by an historian by the name of J. Forbes Munro. In the jacket photograph, Munro's face reflected the same qualities as the "cleric" on the wall in front of me. I had enjoyed his books.

Once I thought of Munro, I remembered a movie credit in gold script, and Respighi's music, and the hushed expectation in the theater. I remembered *Falling Bodies. Screenplay by J. Forbes Munro.*

I exclaimed out loud, "He *couldn't* have written that!"

That was what had been bothering me since Wednesday.

A guard gave me a cautious look and a ten-year-old girl in a school uniform held a finger to her lips and said, "Ssssh!" I grinned at her and ssssh'd her back. I gave Angelico's "Cleric" one last, long look, then turned and walked out of the room.

No, J. Forbes Munro couldn't have written that screenplay. He couldn't have made an obscene joke of the life and work of Galileo, the man he probably revered the most.

Walking back to my office, I thought about what I felt. I didn't think it either true or even possible that Munro had written the screenplay. I had no proof he hadn't. After all, his name was in the credits.

But the idea revolted me. That's what it came to, an emotional response to the idea that Munro had written that screenplay. I didn't know it for certain, and I detest not knowing something for certain.

Three answers were possible: that Munro had indeed written that screenplay; or that he had written one that jibed with my conception of him but it had been turned inside-out by Patrick Player or the studio; or that there was another J. Forbes Munro. Only one of those answers could be true.

Munro had written biographies of Galileo, da Vinci, Thomas More, Erasmus, Martin Luther, John Calvin, Bruno, Savonarola, and the lives of many men of the early Enlightenment. He wrote of these men with such respect—a respect that didn't always include admiration—that one could not help but love or hate the subjects of his biographies.

I had two of Munro's books in my office, one on John Calvin, which I hadn't started yet, and his *Antonio Vivaldi: Pioneer of Harmony*. Like his others, these had been published by Braeden and Brevard here in New York. I didn't bother with their web site but called the office and asked for Munro's editor.

"This is Carol Holvick," a voice answered.

"Tell me," I said, "if I wrote a letter to J. Forbes Munro, care of you or the publisher, could I count on his getting it?"

"Who's this speaking, please?"

"My name is Chess Hanrahan. I've read most of Munro's biography series, and I have some questions for him."

The voice said tentatively, "Well, what kinds of questions? Perhaps I could answer them."

"Do you know of any screenplays he might have written?"

"*Screenplays?*" Mildly incredulous.

"Yes. Screenplays."

I heard a chair squeak. She said, "I'm not aware of any, Mr. Hanrahan." She paused. "Is this the same Chess Hanrahan who—?"

"Yes. The one who shoots diplomats and sends kids to Sing Sing. And the papers won't print the things I do when I'm in a bad mood."

She laughed. "Well, I'm pleased to meet you, Mr. Hanrahan."

"Thank you."

"I'm afraid, though, that Mr. Munro won't be able to satisfy either of our curiosities about screenplays. You see, Mr. Munro is dead."

"Dead."

"Yes. He died about six months ago."

I said, "Oh. . . ."

Chapter 4

"I'm sorry," said Carol Holvick.

I sighed. "Perhaps his agent could answer my question."

"Perhaps he could. Hold on for a moment."

When I heard her voice again, she said, "All his business with us was handled by Friendship and Room. Specifically by Albert Lundy of that agency. I've dealt with Albert for years and I'm sure he'll help you if he can." She gave me the agency's phone number.

"Thank you," I said, writing it down on a legal pad. I thought it was curious that she would have to dig for the name and number of a man she claimed to have dealt with for years, but I didn't pursue the thought because I was too stunned by the news of Munro's death.

"You know," said Holvick, "you could have written him at Ploughsmith College in Queens. He taught there for years and they would have forwarded a letter to his widow."

The jacket bio beneath his picture said that Munro taught European history at Ploughsmith. I would have tried that route in time, but I was after a quick answer. I said as much to Holvick.

"What makes you think he wrote screenplays, Mr. Hanrahan?" the editor asked.

"A movie I saw recently. You said he died six months ago. When, exactly?"

"Last April. Early April. It was on all the front pages."

"I was out of town," I said. In fact, in early April I was in Paris, on a two-week drive around the Continent, revisiting all the sights my parents had shown me when I was five. "How did he die?"

"Why, he was mugged. Someone held him up in Central Park, then beat him to death."

Again I said, "Oh. . . ." I asked, "Did the police catch anyone?"

"I don't think so. I couldn't say for sure. We haven't heard any more about it."

"Well, thanks for your help. I'll call again if I have any more questions."

"If you find out about screenplays, let me know. You can stop up any time. I'd be thrilled to meet you. Perhaps I could talk you into writing a book about your cases." Holvick paused. "Are you . . . on a case, Mr. Hanrahan?"

"No. I'm something of a fan of Munro's, that's all."

Damn, I thought as I replaced the receiver. Mugged and murdered in Central Park. I picked up the receiver again and dialed Friendship and Room, Literary Agents. Mr. Lundy was out of the office and not expected back until later in the afternoon. It was three-thirty now. I left a message with the operator, not expecting him back at all late on a Friday afternoon. I watered my plants and browsed Munro's biography of Calvin. At five to four, Lundy returned my call. "How can I help you . . . Mr. Hanrahan, is it? I can barely read this person's handwriting."

"That's right," I said. I told him who had referred me to him and why, and asked, "Are you aware of any screenplays he might have written?"

"Screenplays? Why, no, I'm not. We've represented Mr. Munro for twenty or so years, and I don't recollect anything like that at all."

"That wouldn't rule out the possibility that he wrote one?"

"No, of course not. But he never brought it up in conversation. And if he wrote screenplays, we wouldn't necessarily see them, either. That's another business altogether and he would have had to use a Hollywood agent."

"I see."

"Mr. Munro was a very private person," said Lundy. "He was a distinguished historian and also a professor of classics. His biography series was something of a sideline for him, because he was primarily a teacher."

"Did you know him well?"

"No, not at all. I probably know only a little more about him than you. He came from a fairly wealthy family. He turned down invitations to join the faculties of two Ivy League schools, and we learned that only because of academic gossip from a few of our other author clients. When he died, we were surprised to learn that he'd been married. I've met her, and concluded some of her husband's business with her. But otherwise we've only dealt with her through her attorneys, who guard her identity."

"I see," I said again. I asked, "May I have his widow's address?"

"I'm afraid I can't give you that information, Mr. Hanrahan. Not without Mrs. Munro's or her attorney's permission. Her instructions on that point—via her attorney—are quite clear. We would lose the Munro estate as a client if we violated that confidence." Lundy paused, then spoke before I could. "I can give you the name of her attorney, of course."

"All right."

"Siskind, Dietz and Tigrini. John Tigrini is the attorney who represents her. Here's his number."

I wrote that down, too.

Lundy cleared his throat. "Of course, you may also write her care of Ploughsmith College. He taught history there for fifteen years. I'm sure the school will forward your query. You might even sound out his former colleagues there."

"Yes, I'd thought of that," I said. "I'm just trying to keep this simple." I paused. "Tell me, has anyone else ever approached you on this matter?"

"No, we've never been involved in that kind of business. I'd be very much surprised if we were approached. Mr. Munro's work hardly lends itself to it, except if someone wanted to make a documentary about one of his subjects."

I said thanks and goodbye, and dialed the phone one last time. But Mr. Tigrini of Siskind, Dietz and Tigrini had gone out of town, and no one else there would be able to help me locate Munro's widow.

If I wrote to Munro's widow care of her attorneys, I might get a reply in weeks or months, if there was a reply at all. My name could simply scare off the legal beagles. I thought it shouldn't be so hard to get a simple answer. I had a *Who's Who* on my office shelf and I pulled it out. I lit a cigarette and turned the pages.

There! J. (Jarvis) Forbes Munro. Born twenty years before I was. American biographer, essayist, lecturer, teacher. Son of Brian and Joyce (*née* Forbes) Munro. Born in Seattle. Et cetera, et cetera. My finger glided to the last lines of the entry. Damn! Address, care of Friendship and Room, Literary Agents, 1060 Madison Avenue, New York.

I slammed the volume shut and put it aside. Ploughsmith College. I dismissed the idea. It was after five o'clock. There was no point in making another call.

Then I remembered that the jacket of one of Munro's books— one I had at home—had a picture of him standing outside somewhere, along with a brief but different bio. I tried to recall what it said but couldn't. He had to have lived somewhere. I checked the net. There were dozens of Munros in the New York boroughs and Long Island but not a single J. Forbes Munro.

I closed the office and went home, taking the two Munro books with me. After I'd freshened up and fed Walker, my big, long-legged orange tabby, I hunted up the other books in my library.

I was right. All but one jacket featured the head-and-shoulders shot of Munro—the image that resembled Fra Angelico's "Cleric"—with some bookshelves slightly out of focus behind him. The exception was the jacket of a biography of Martin Luther, published over ten years ago, which showed a three-quarter length photograph taken of him standing on a street. In the background were some blurred buildings—a church, an apartment building, and a lot of trees and landscaped greenery—and a small park. But those things weren't what tickled my memory. It was the lampposts lining the street behind him. They were the old-fashioned gaslight kind, with four corners of sloped glass fixed to an iron brace atop a baroquely ornamented iron post, crowned by an ornate lid. I had seen those recently but couldn't place them. There were three visible in the picture, indistinct but recognizable. They weren't city lampposts. Where had I seen them?

I looked at the photo credit: Bobbi Cabot. Was she a professional photographer or just a friend or relative of Munro's? And would she remember having taken his picture ten or more years ago? The background reminded me of an English town—Surrey—I'd passed through last April, a cluster of pre-war brick Tudor-style homes and townhouses. Around its single landscaped square were stores and shops, including a teashop in which I'd had my first and last ever watercress sandwich.

What I thought of as "pre-war" in this case was pre-World War I. The place had reminded me of a suburb right here in New York, built by some philanthropist before that war and intended to be country housing for the lower middle class. That was when the suburb wasn't a suburb at all, but mostly pasture and field.

And then I remembered where I'd seen those lampposts. In

Queens. Forest Hills Gardens. The suburb that time forgot. Except that no middle class lived there now, if one ever had. The Gardens was still a private development, but the only people who owned houses or rented apartments there today were people in very high income brackets. I glanced at the Bobbi Cabot photo again. It only whetted my curiosity.

I looked out the window. It was too dark to head out there now, but I was certain that tomorrow morning I could identify the background of that photograph.

Just under a year ago I'd gone to Forest Hills Gardens on a social call. Old friends of my father had invited me to dinner in their townhouse on Burns Street. Saturday morning I drove the Mercedes out there and parked just off Queens Boulevard, walked beneath a Long Island Railroad overpass and entered the Gardens.

The shock was both esthetic and auditory. It was like stepping back in time. It was quiet. The trees were tall, thick and old. The buildings were well-kept. I came onto a quaint little square—almost identical to the one in Old Putnam, Surrey, England—where several buildings were connected by overhead pedestrian bridges. Every structure, including the bridges, had a red tile roof. The square was bounded by the bridges, two of them leading to the railroad station on the overpass. And, of course, there were the lampposts. I took out the book jacket I'd brought with me and compared the ones in the photograph with the ones in the square.

Yes, this was the place. Nice place for an historian to live, if he wanted to be frozen in time.

Four streets radiated from the square. I tried to remember which street was Burns and which bridge I'd passed under to reach it a year ago. I chose one and got thoroughly lost. It was a pleasant way to get lost. It was only nine in the morning and no one was about to help me.

I retraced my steps back to the square and struck out in another direction. Once past the bridge, I found myself at a fork,

Greenway North and Greenway South. I took Greenway North. Soon I began to recognize things from the dust jacket picture. Then, a block away, I saw the church and the apartment building. I crossed the park that divided North and South, and I looked back.

This was it. The photograph had been taken on Greenway South. Everything was there: the buildings, the trees, the shrubbery, the lampposts. The picture had even been taken about the same time of year, in late autumn. Along the sidewalk on Greenway South was an ivy-grown brick wall. Some of the townhouses had gates, others didn't. But they all had mailboxes, with the street number and the resident's name on the sides. I walked along and read the names. And came upon one that read *J. Forbes Munro. No. 29.*

He had been photographed about half a block away from the gate to his house. I folded the book jacket, tucked it inside my coat pocket, then opened the gate to No. 29 and walked up the flagstone steps to a thick oaken door. The upstairs windows had drawn curtains, but to the left I could see into what appeared to be a bookcase-lined study. Piano music came faintly from the lead-paned glass. I recognized the notes from Schumann's "Scenes from Childhood." I pushed the button beside the door.

I waited. The recording was stopped, and I glanced to my left just in time to catch sight of an indistinct figure leaving the window after scrutinizing me. Then the door opened. When the face registered in my mind, I was too stunned to gasp.

Mrs. J. Forbes Munro. Formerly Kimberly Eames.

Chapter 5

There was a moment of shared recognition that had nothing to do with our respective careers, a pleasant moment, and we set about denying it.

I said, "Mrs. Munro?"

"Yes?"

"My name is Chess Hanrahan. I'd like to ask you some questions about your late husband."

An involuntary smile bent her lips. "So, it's true, what they said about you."

"What's that?"

"That there's no refusing you an answer, once you've asked a question."

It wasn't true, but I wouldn't have minded if people thought so. "Who delivered that insight?"

"The people who warned me yesterday about you. They were certain that you couldn't find me. They thought there were too many obstacles."

"I see."

"They were wrong."

"The obstacles didn't amount to much," I said. "May I come in and ask you some questions?"

She shook her head. "No, Mr. Hanrahan. I've pledged myself to silence on any matter concerning my late husband. It's my best defense against curiosity. Please don't take it personally."

And before I knew it, I was staring at a closed door.

I raised a hand to press the doorbell again—not so much in anger with being cut off as not to lose sight of her—but dropped my arm. I opened my mouth to say something, but there was nothing to say and no one to say it to. I turned, went back down the flagstone steps, opened the gate, and gently closed it behind me. Dividing the triangular park between the two Greenways was a little circular area with benches on its rim that faced inward. I crossed the street and wandered up to it, then sat down on a bench that faced the square beyond the trees.

On my second cigarette I was able to think clearly about what had happened. I had seen something in her eyes that I couldn't identify but didn't like. Not resignation, nor despair. Numbness, I thought. All the way down on the bottom rung of negation.

I turned my head to look at her house, and there she was again, halfway across the street, in slacks and a dark overcoat, her hands buried deeply in its side pockets. I studied her brow and eyelashes and grim mouth and the chestnut hair that stirred in the breeze of her movement as she came closer. She paused by the circle. There was no smile on her face, only an impersonal interest in my presence. I said nothing and waited.

"Forbes and I used to sit here," she said. "We'd go out on long walks through all the neighborhoods in the Gardens. We'd have such a wonderful time talking that when we got back, we'd sit here for a while and say nothing to each other, because we didn't want it to end. He called this little circle our 'punctuation mark.' I don't like other people to sit here."

"He meant that much to you."

"He was simply the best I'd ever seen or known, a measure of manhood . . . close to the top. I think I meant the same thing to him. He didn't try to be less than what he was. That's why I loved him. He was a hero—not in all ways but in enough ways to make him exceptional. He never once tried to belittle himself or me or his work."

The sound of an express train on the railroad tracks approached, swelled to a racket, rocketed by, and faded as it hurtled toward Manhattan.

"That is important," I said.

She was sitting now, on the same bench, on the other end of the curve. Frowning at me, she asked, "Why do *you* say it's important?"

"It's the norm for men to diminish themselves. It takes courage to resist wanting to join in."

She asked, "How *did* you find me, Mr. Hanrahan?"

I told her about the photograph of Munro.

"You're a private investigator. Are you acting on someone's behalf?"

"Just my own."

"Why?"

"I saw a movie recently that credited your husband with the screenplay."

She automatically began to say the words, but couldn't pronounce them. Her eyes closed.

"*Falling Bodies*," I said.

Her eyes opened. "Forbes did not write that screenplay. What about it?"

I lit another cigarette. "I didn't think he had."

"Why not?"

"Because then he couldn't have written any of his books." I watched he, trying to guess what was going on. "I'll tell you the kind of person who could have. In my senior year of high school there was a kid named Chet Biddle. He was the school's top gymnast; won a dozen awards and a college scholarship. At our senior prom, he did handstands and kept walking across the dance floor upside-down to look up the girls' gowns. That's the kind of person who could have written that screenplay."

After a moment she said, "You must despise me for having appeared in the film."

"I don't think so."

She stood up with decision. "Do yourself and me a favor," she said. "Don't think of me as 'Mrs. Munro' or as the widow of a man you obviously respect. Think of me as Kimberly Eames, an actress who was less than she appeared and whom you should despise. And then forget me, forget that film, and whatever else you may think is wrong. It's senseless to go on caring about what can't be undone."

I faced her. "You're obviously not practicing what you preach."

She looked away from me. "I'm required to do penance. You're not. Please keep it that way." She turned and took a step to go.

I said, "*Is* it penance you're doing?"

"How can you doubt it?"

"'Despair is a corrosive,'" I said, quoting. "'Its acids eat away at everything one could possibly value, until one can no longer care for anything, ever again.'" I smiled a little at her frown of recollection. It was the line that had made her famous, a line from her only suspense picture.

She moved away into the street. A moment later she was back inside the house.

Chapter 6

I left the Gardens and walked to my car on Austin Street, outside her world. I was only vaguely aware of the traffic and the swarms of Saturday morning shoppers.

That line I'd used she had delivered to an F.B.I. agent in *Fraction of Fear*, a suspense picture set in World War II New York. She wore a long fur coat and a Forties-style toque, and she stood on one of the parapets that overlooked the East River. She was glancing back into the night at her future tormenter, the Federal agent who was also a Nazi agent, who would later try to blackmail her into stealing her scientist husband's secret wartime research on air-to-surface rocket propellant.

Her over-the-shoulder pose had been used in the print ads for the picture. Coupled with the title, it was an eye-catching combination. The film did well at the box office. It shouldn't have, because the story was flat and full of plot holes. But Kimberly Eames's presence had given the picture a life it didn't deserve.

I shuddered at the thought of her being on the same set with

Elliott Rhodes, the other lead in that picture. Rhodes had been a screen idol of mine until I was in high school. Then both his character and physical appearance had decayed. I'd learned later that he was a short-tempered alcoholic who had been arrested for beating two now-divorced wives and assaulting a waiter. In *Fraction of Fear* I'd had my most recent chance to take a look at him, as he'd played the Federal-turned-Nazi agent.

Where was I when I saw it? I was at the end of my first year as chief of police in East Auberley, Massachusetts, a university town. A quiet town, not unlike Forest Hills Gardens. A safe place to hide, if that was one's purpose. It demanded nothing and offered no risks. I'd been there licking my wounds, slow to understand that I had to go back to New York.

I wondered if Kimberly Eames had found a similar refuge out here. And wondered if I could—or should—jolt her out of it.

I stopped by my apartment on Sixty-eighth and picked up a notebook, then dropped by the Midtown East precinct station to see if Lieutenant James Navarro was on duty in Homicide. We'd met during a serial murder case, which I'd cracked, and he didn't seem to hold that against me. He was in his office, glanced at me disgustedly, and said, as a warning, "I came in just to get some paperwork out of the way." He pushed an ashtray he rarely used in my direction across his file-laden desk. "If this is a social call, then I'll forgive you. If it's business, God help you."

"Half and half," I said, sitting down in a corner chair and unbuttoning my coat. "Working hard?"

"Harder than you." He sipped coffee from a blue mug with the NYPD coat of arms on the side. "Which half do you want to bother me with first?"

I lit a cigarette. "Some time ago I discovered a writer. More precisely, a biographer. He wrote about the lives of famous men. He was a bit famous himself. I learned yesterday that he died. I know how. That doesn't interest me as much, but I am curious about it."

"Who's this writer?" Navarro asked.

"J. Forbes Munro."

Navarro grimaced. "Oh. Him."

"Any progress? Or weren't you involved in the investigation?"

"Oh, I was involved, all right. And I can tell you we haven't moved an inch on it. Probably never will. What's your interest?"

I shrugged. "It isn't every day that biographers are murdered in Central Park. I was out of town last April when it happened."

"Stop dodging, Chess. What's your interest?"

I grinned. "Sheer curiosity. That's all."

"Yeah, you liked his books. You read a lot." He was too tired to pretend he believed me. "All right: We tried like hell to find his killer—or killers. Checked all the parolees and other predators we have files on. Zip. Not even extra help from downtown made a dent. We're not magicians."

"Granted."

"The file's still open, collecting dust. It'll be closed in another year and sent downtown. It would've been nice if we'd been able to nail someone. The brass would've loved us. Might've even sprung for new desks and equipment for the precinct."

"No witnesses? No leads at all?"

"Nope. He may as well have been zapped by invisible aliens. We went all over his life a month before he died—that was dull reading—and Forensics even put the asphalt we found him on under the microscope. Zip, again."

"Why the extra help? He wasn't a mayor's aide. Just another teacher."

Navarro smiled, and I saw the light.

"Kimberly Eames."

Navarro put his coffee mug down. "How in hell . . . ?"

"I spoke with her not over two hours ago. In person."

"She hire you to put your nose—?"

"No one's hired me to nose into anything."

"So you talked to her."

"We talked. What did you make of her?"

"She didn't want publicity. When the captain drafted extra help, I was told to check her alibi. It's the first thing we got out of the way. She was on a plane that night, coming back from a visit to her parents in Chicago. She couldn't have done it anyway. Munro was about your size. There wasn't any reason we could see. We didn't think she'd hired someone to flatten him, either."

"What else?"

Navarro shrugged. "We didn't know who Mrs. Munro was until I went out to question her in Forest Hills. That kind of thing—the missing celebrity secretly married—word gets around fast. The brass heard about it, but they played it smart for a change, didn't shoot off their mouths about how we're going to nail the murderer of a movie star's spouse in half an hour. We'd warned them we had nothing to go on, so they kept it quiet."

"So the headlines Munro got didn't mention her?"

"That's it. It was all in the late editions of the papers. She came down here just once, to sign a statement. Not much work got done around here then. A lot of the guys were torn between leaving her alone and asking for her autograph. But they left her alone. There's something strange about that woman. Attractive and put-offish. Once you get past all the glamour—and I wasn't certain I did—there's something powerful about her. She'd look at me and make me want to ask her when she'd like dinner ready or what could I get her from Tiffany's. That look," said Navarro with a sigh.

He noticed something in my expression, grinned with satisfaction. "My God, even the great Chess Hanrahan isn't immune to her."

I said, "How was Munro found?"

"Mounted patrol going through the Park just before dawn, looking for bums who'd spent their last nickels in the night. Can't have the citizens tripping over deceased vagrants, you know."

"Where in the Park?"

"Under a foot bridge near the duck pond."

"His editor—that's who told me all about this—said he'd been beaten to death."

"That's a mild description of his condition. His skull had been kicked in, all but three of his ribs smashed. Even his glasses got it, a rimless pair with real glass, stomped to smithereens. There were glass particles in his eyes. All his belongings were taken—watch, wallet, pens, cash, his briefcase. We recovered most of it except for the cash and his keys. It was all tossed in the bushes. Whoever did it just didn't like him and beat him to death. Maybe he talked back or fought back. Officially, we even doubt that robbery was the original motive. It stands as a psycho kill. He shouldn't have been walking alone in the Park at that time of night. But he did, and he ran into a nut. We half expected to find his cash in the bushes, too."

"What was he doing there?"

"He was attending some historical association's conference going on that weekend in a nearby hotel, the Tivoli Towers. It was the first night of the conference. Munro gave a speech to a general meeting and was on one of that day's panels. We found a draft of his speech and his panel notes with everything else the killer had scattered. The widow identified it all, books, a calculator, pens, pencils, address book, restaurant menu, credit cards. We returned the stuff to her. None of it was any use to us."

"Well," I said, checking my watch and rising. "I've got a date with Patience and Fortitude."

"Who?"

"My favorite lions at Fifth and Forty-second."

"Oh, the Library." Navarro feigned disgust. "What kind of detective are you anyway, hanging around books all the time."

It didn't take me long to collect all I could find on Kimberly Eames at the Library. That's how brief her career had been, four pictures. There were a few articles in magazines I couldn't count on finding online. I copied them, then looked around on web sites. I could do the same work at my office, but I liked the Library, liked the idea of strata of knowledge buried here and the image of myself and the people around me as patient archaeologists.

I collected reviews of Eames's pictures from three different newspapers and a few magazines. There was a feature article on the effect she had on the movie-goers. There was a magazine interview of her that was alternately fawning and patronizing. But I gradually got a picture of her background.

She grew up in Chicago, was a top student at a private high school, and dropped out of college in her first year. She appeared in print ads for Chicago department stores, modeled clothes for another store's mail order catalogue, and was sent to Europe several times to model American fashion designs.

She moved to New York, worked odd jobs while studying acting at two drama schools. She found work in cosmetics commercials, modeled at private fashion shows, and was a sometime "cover girl" for two women's magazines. She was the "Magellan Woman" in the Lefcourt and Sons Wine Company champagne commercials on television—I remembered that campaign well—and appeared in bit parts Off-Broadway. While in the role of Amanda in a Connecticut summer theater production of Coward's *Private Lives*, she was "discovered" by an assistant director with Excelsior Films. A year later, in a support role in *Savoy 9000,* she was hailed by critics as the best thing to come out of Hollywood in years. She did three more pictures, including *Falling Bodies,* and then dropped out of sight.

Mention of Kimberly Eames ceased. Speculation about her future plans evaporated. Other cast members of *Falling Bodies* were written up, but not Eames. There was no mention of her marriage to Munro, no curiosity about her whereabouts. The abrupt and consistent absence of any mention of her name in all those publications—after a certain date—gave me an uneasy feeling. It was as though critics, career watchers and gossip columnists were relieved she was gone.

I had planned to research J. Forbes Munro, too, but the

Library closed at five on Saturdays and I ran out of time. I stuck the stack of printouts and photocopies inside my notebook and was the last patron the guard shooed out the door.

I stood for a while at the bottom of the Library's steps, next to Patience. Patrick Player, Eames's co-star in *Falling Bodies*, was in town in *something*—I'd been seeing his name every other day in ads on the *Times* theater page—and I wanted to talk to him. I crossed Fifth Avenue, headed down to Grand Central and bought a *Times* at a newsstand. There it was, toward the end of a column of boxes. *Trackside*, by Paul Gandling, starring Patrick Player. At the Gilpin Theater on Twelfth Street. Now in its fourth smash month. "Hilarious!" read a blurb from a national news magazine. "An express you'll never catch!" punned a famous drama critic.

I went downstairs and took the shuttle to Times Square. At the discount ticket outlet on Broadway, I bought a ticket to *Trackside*.

Chapter 7

The Gilpin Theater was on Twelfth Street on the western fringe of the Village. It had once been a small movie house. The overhead marquee and unused jukebox-like ticket booth beneath it were all that had survived renovation. There were photos of Patrick Player and the rest of the cast and blown-up reviews of *Trackside* behind the glass displays. The lobby was crammed with people talking and drinking coffee and wine. There were no lines, though clots of people kept coming up and going in. At the door, an usher tore my ticket in half and gave me a program. I made my way through the crowd to the small auditorium.

Once I was settled in my seat, I opened the program and turned to the cast list. There were about twenty names. I glanced up at the curtained stage. Twenty people could be fitted on it, but not before scenery and props were removed first. There were no character names. Patrick Player was listed as Commuter No. 1, Anne Volney as Commuter No. 2, Selby Lane as Commuter No. 3, and so on. Then there were a Trackworker, a Dispatcher, a Purse Snatcher, and a Tin Cup. The Tin Cup, said a note at the bottom, was played in alternating performances by Milton Prosser and Myra Sloat.

I leafed to the production and cast credits. Paul Gandling, the playwright, among other things had also written *Nidus* and *Queen Francine*, both of which had begun as Off-Broadway plays and ended as Hollywood releases. "The commercial success of some of my earlier work," wrote Gandling in the program notes, "has enabled me to devote more time to serious dramaturgy." If I recalled correctly, *Nidus* had been an ecological horror picture—something about insects revolting against man and his pesticides—while *Queen Francine* had been a parody of the "screwball" comedy genre of the Thirties. I'd seen the latter, ages ago. It hadn't been very funny. Patrick Player had starred in both films.

When I read Player's credit, some of the mystery of why he was appearing in an Off-Broadway play cleared in my mind: he and Gandling went back together many years. Gandling, a scriptwriter who kept to topical issues, was passing himself off now—with a little help from the critics—as a "serious" playwright. Player had appeared in Gandling's early Hollywood releases, when everyone thought his career was all but finished. Something tickled my memory. I thought—as people took their seats around me and the place got hotter and noisier—that I should take a deeper look at Player's career.

At eight o'clock, the lights dimmed and the curtain swept aside to reveal a set that was a reproduction of an above-ground passenger platform in the Bronx. It was faithfully detailed: litter on the oil-spotted platform, crushed cans, Styrofoam containers, candy wrappers, cigarette butts, discarded newspapers, overflowing trash can. Graffiti marred the steel pillars and an information booth. Some of the letters on the Northbound and Southbound signs overhead had been blacked out. There were six neon lights on the roof; two of them worked, and a third flickered in slow death. In the background was a realistically painted representation of South Bronx tenements, with boarded-up windows and fire-blackened brick walls. The set was elevated so that you could see a little beneath the platform; there was dirty gravel, more litter, a length of steel rail, and mechanical rats that would pop out and scurry with squeals into another hole under the platform.

And somehow—and this seemed to give the audience a thrill—they had rigged it up so that the set even exuded the smells associated with a semi-derelict station. The total effect was grimy depression.

The first Commuter—Patrick Player, as a nattily dressed businessman with a briefcase—mounted the stage from stairs not visible to the audience and rushed up to the uniformed employee in the information booth. "Is the express to Poughkeepsie running?" he asked in a panic. "Nah, it's crawling," answered the gum-chewing, hostile Dispatcher. That got a laugh from the audience, and the play was off and running. Or crawling.

In no time Player was joined by other commuters, who wandered on and off the platform in a series of plots and subplots I could make no sense of. I got the drift of the story ten minutes into the first act. It was an existential statement—capital E optional—about the meaninglessness and meanness of modern life. The express trains which all the commuters were waiting for never came, or kept breaking down offstage, or were rerouted to another line. The commuters got into arguments and fights with each other and with the Dispatcher, they watched the Trackworker sabotage the vending machines, they beat up the Purse Snatcher, and generally made fools of themselves and of each other.

Patrick Player, as Commuter No. 1, had the best lines, such as they were, including, "The world is made up of the vulgar," which I thought was lifted from Machiavelli. Act One ended with the entrance of the Tin Cup, an incredibly filthy creature whom one could also smell. He crawled up from his home under the platform with his tin cup. He didn't say much before the curtain closed, but I was willing to bet that in Act Two he would enlighten both the commuters and the audience with his wisdom, moral conscience, and special karma.

I wasn't fast enough and got stuck in the crowd making its thirsty way to the concession stand. I managed to grab a coffee and went outside for some fresh air and a smoke. I tried to think about the play, but my mind was a blank. There was little to think about. I went back inside and elbowed my way through animated chatter and asked around for the stage manager. One of the concession people pointed out an anxious-looking woman who stood near a door marked "Private Office." I walked up to her, introduced myself, and asked if it was possible to see Patrick Player after the show.

"I'm afraid Mr. Player will be leaving immediately after the performance, sir," she said with practiced indifference.

"It's business," I said with a smile, and pulled out my wallet. I flipped it open so she could see my old Police Department I.D. in one window, and the gold shield of the chief of police of police of East Auberley facing it. "Nothing serious," I assured her, "but there are some questions I'd like to ask him. After the show is fine. It'll take only a minute."

"Well," replied the stage manager, all attention now, "I'll ask, but I can't promise anything."

"Thanks," I said, putting my wallet away. "Tell him it's about J. Forbes Munro. He'll understand." I paused, then decided to rib her. "Interesting play. Wonderful set. The rats give it special authenticity. Too bad you couldn't have trained some flies to swarm around that trash can. Maybe even some bees."

She surprised me. Her face brightened. "You know, the set designer suggested that *very thing*! But we didn't think it would quite work, and anyway, there's a health ordinance. I'll be right back." She disappeared into the auditorium.

I stood by the office door and listened to the intermission talk. Most of it rattled approvingly about the play, but one old man, who looked as though he'd been dragged here by his wife, said with a defensive scowl, "If this Gandling fellow had put half as much thought into the story as someone did into that set, well, maybe he'd have realized there was no story!" To which the woman beside him replied, "Jerald, don't be so critical. It's so *true* what goes on up there. Why, just the other day, when I was waiting for the Flushing train . . ."

The stage manager returned, said in a low voice, "Mr. Hanrahan, Mr. Player said he would be delighted to see you after the performance, but only for a few moments, since he has an engagement to go to."

"Thanks."

"If you'd wait here after the final curtain, I'll come for you and take you backstage to his dressing room." She paused shyly. "I didn't know you were *the* Chess Hanrahan, and Mr. Player didn't realize you were a fan of his."

I hadn't said I was a fan of Player's, and I wondered why the actor would be delighted to see me.

"I'll be here," I said.

Before the lights dimmed again, I noticed that there were more empty seats than at the first curtain. I was right about the Tin Cup. By the last curtain, after long and profane speeches, he'd persuaded several commuters to trade their gray flannels for sackcloth—or whatever it was he was wearing—and had talked others into jumping off the platform to certain death below. When he disappeared again under the tracks, taking his new converts with him, only Patrick Player remained on stage, his suit in tatters, clutching his mangled briefcase, sitting stubbornly on an overturned vending machine, waiting for the express. It was a poignant scene, if you were ignorant of the Absurdist dialectical symbolism. Or perhaps it was poignant if you weren't. The audience applauded anyway. Many in it probably regretted that the set itself couldn't take a bow with the cast.

Five minutes later I was ushered into the tiny room backstage. Patrick Player sat at a dressing table, in a robe, hurriedly removing his makeup.

He was a tall man, as tall as his pictures portrayed him. He grinned at me through his mirror as he used a rag and some chemical to clean his face. It was a lean face with frank, intelligent blue eyes, high cheekbones, and a nose that wasn't quite Roman. He moved in a manner radically different from his stage manner, which this evening had been brusque and jerky. Watching him now, he was one of the few men I knew who could still project unquestionable masculinity with a studied, efficient grace. "Ah, the sly Mr. Hanrahan. Welcome, sir! Thank you, Doris. And, Doris . . ."

"Yes, Mr. Player?" the stage manager answered.

"Make sure your props person fixes the trick arm of my suit jacket. It came off just a little too easily in Mr. Lane's hands in the third fight scene. It's supposed to *tear* off—loudly enough for the audience to hear it—not slip silently off my arm like a silk glove. All right?"

Doris took the tattered suit off a coat rack. The trick sleeve was tucked neatly into the hole of the shoulder. "It'll be ready by tomorrow, Mr. Player." She flashed a smile at me and left the dressing room.

Player gave a brief turn of his head to me. "What can I do for you?"

"Thank you for seeing me, Mr. Player," I said. "I have only one question: Who wrote the screenplay for *Falling Bodies*?"

Player grinned into the mirror. "Who wrote the screenplay…? What an odd question. I—"

There was a knock on the door, and it opened. A man in his twenties in a dark suit leaned in long enough to say, "Mr. Player, the car's just outside when you're ready."

"Thanks, Bob. I shouldn't be more than five minutes."

The door closed. Player frowned. "Frankly, Mr. Hanrahan, I can't remember just this minute. I'd have to ask around or look at my records to see who actually worked on that script."

"I can tell you who couldn't have written it, even though his name is in the credits," I said. "J. Forbes Munro."

Player paused in his task and looked thoughtful. "Ah! Now there's a name I haven't heard in years! And now my mind begins to clear. It *was* Forbes Munro. I believe it was collaboration. Can't recall the other writer's name, however."

I said, "Kimberly Eames denies that Munro had anything to do with it."

"Kimberly! Another name from the past! Our truant goddess! I heard she's hung out a scutcheon of silence."

"So it would seem."

"You . . . know what a scutcheon is?"

"Sure," I said. "I do crossword puzzles."

Player laughed, and turned to face me for a short study. He wagged a finger at me. "You know, I read a book recently by an education expert in which he claimed that if modern high school students were required to complete one crossword puzzle a day, our literacy rate would skyrocket." He turned back to the table to remove the last patches of grease paint from his face.

I shrugged. "It couldn't have been written by Munro."

"I couldn't say, sir. Can't remember that fellow's name, either." Player paused. "You know, a script is never finished until it's in the can. Shot and signed off by the director. Everyone works on it until the final take. Then it's the editor's turn. What else did Miss Eames say, other than that?"

"Not much more."

"I can have an absolute answer for you in no time," said Player. He frowned. "But—why are you so interested in whether or not Munro wrote that particular screenplay?"

"I don't believe he did, that's all." I added, "It's not his style."

Player rose and went to a washbasin in the corner. He lathered up some soap and scrubbed his face, then dried briskly with a towel. He paused to study me again. "You're probably wondering: What on earth am *I* doing *here*? Well, I'm taking a vacation from the camera. My acting skills need honing. The stage will sharpen them for any actor who has talent." After another pause, he added, "You needn't have shown Doris half a dozen badges of authority to see me, Mr. Hanrahan. Just your name would have done the trick."

"I showed her the badge to get her attention," I said. "I don't take my notoriety for granted. Not everyone reads newspapers."

"True. But I do. And even though your name has appeared infrequently in the press, I recognized it instantly." Player slipped out of his robe, and as he pulled down a turtleneck sweater, he asked, "Are you on a case?"

"No. This is a matter of personal curiosity."

Player shook his head. "'Personal curiosity.' How benign a motive! I believe you were quoted in some gossip column here that most of your cases begin with it. Perhaps I shouldn't be speaking with you. I might find myself stammering an alibi."

He was referring to Ellen Romero's interview with me that had appeared in her Manhattan *Chronicle* column about four months ago. It had taken up only ten lines and was lost among the other tidbits she'd picked up at the same restaurant anniversary party I'd attended. I marveled at Player's memory. I said, "Not if you've nothing to hide."

"I don't, not in regards to Forbes Munro. At least, I don't think I do. Terrible way for him to die. I sent Kimberly a card, but she never acknowledged it." Player went back to the table and brushed his generous mane of black and silver-streaked hair. He put the brush down and smiled thoughtfully, then turned to me. His face brightened. "I've just had an idea! I have a proposition to offer you, but I don't want to make it until after I've talked with some colleagues. Tell me, what are you doing next Wednesday evening?"

"Nothing special. Why?"

Player glanced at a clock on the table. "No doubt you've heard of Elaine Card's big mental disease bash at the Waldorf next week. It's been publicized loudly enough. I'll be there. I can get you invited—or have you already been?"

"I was, but I declined."

Player looked gaily contrite. "Devious of me to put it to you that way. I must confess that I'm sure I saw your name on her invitee list. I'm only an honorary chairman of the event, but I was sent a list for vetting."

I shook my head. "I'm not a giving man."

"You don't look like Richard the Third, either," chuckled Player. "Well, in that case, I'm hosting a post-banquet party at my place on Long Island. At Soundview."

I recalled both Soundview and the line from *Richard the Third* made famous by another noted actor and which, slighted altered, I'd unconsciously fed Player, who'd punned it on cue. "I'd heard that some preservation outfit owned Soundview."

"*I* am chairman of that outfit, Mr. Hanrahan. I don't live there, of course. To keep it habitable would require the budget of the San Diego Zoo. It was my grandfather's. He won it off a banker who could hold neither his liquor nor his real estate, in a poker game. That was back in the Twenties, long before I was born. I lived there for a while, as a child, when my father wasn't on the road or shooting on location. Well, the tourists can have it."

Player reached into an open closet and took out a jacket and camel hair coat. As he put them on, he said, "But my party will start some time after the dinner in town here. Would you come? There'll be three or four hundred guests—not including the press—so you'll need an invitation to present at the door. I wouldn't want to see you bounced as a crasher. I can have one sent to your office by messenger on Monday. Please say you'll come. I think you'll be intrigued by my proposition." Player paused. "I can even promise you a definite answer about the authorship of that screenplay."

I suspected that I was being set up somehow. The answer I wanted should have been at the tip of his tongue. But my suspicion only piqued my curiosity. "All right. Tux?"

"Black tie. Bring a friend. I think you'll enjoy yourself." Player patted his pockets, and buttoned up his coat. "You're in the directory? Of course. Oh! By the way—how did you like the play?"

He hadn't answered my question yet, and I might have reason to ask him another in the future. So I said, "Why aren't you doing Shakespeare, or some late contemporary, or someone worthy of your talent?"

Player's eyes held shrewd recognition of my true answer. "Will you walk me to my car?" he said.

He said goodnight to cast members who hadn't left yet and to Doris. We exited by a side door into an alley. Lighting a cigarette, he said, "Shakespeare? A 'late contemporary'—no doubt a euphemism for the writer of a well-made play! I think I know your tastes, Mr. Hanrahan. You can't fool me. Good grief, I'd do Shakespeare or one of your late contemporaries at the drop of a hat! Have done it, as a matter of fact. Long ago, on the straw hat circuit. I did a fairly famous *Hamlet* and *Richard the Third* and *Lear*. I love the stage. So, why don't I do it now? Because, you see, it's very difficult these days to find a cast literate enough to do such fare—or an audience that could appreciate it. Well, here's my car." We stopped by a silver limousine; the door was being held open by the chauffeur. Player took my hand and shook it. "Good night, Mr. Hanrahan. I look forward to seeing you next Wednesday."

I needed a drink and a solid meal. I was exhausted. Acting didn't come naturally to me. I may as well have been lifting barbells the whole time I was in the Gilpin Theater. It was a strain to force yourself to tolerate the presence of a man you'd sooner flatten than have patronize you. Player was no dummy. He wasn't so wrapped up in himself as to believe he evoked either awe or adulation in me.

He had something else in mind.

A proposition.

Chapter 8

My last thought before my mind winked out that night was that it was curious that Patrick Player hadn't asked me *why* I didn't think Munro had written the screenplay.

And my first thought on Sunday morning was that it certainly *was* curious. The picture that almost won him an Academy Award. I didn't believe he couldn't recall the name of the screenwriter.

He didn't ask the right question, yet he'd invited me to a party.

I stood at my picture window in the living room with my coffee and a cigarette and watched it rain outside. I wondered what Kimberly Eames did on such mornings. What was she doing now? She ought to be living in Manhattan, not in Forest Hills, stuck in time. I ought to be able to see the lights of her apartment from here, on top of one of those towers.

It was nice if she could see the lights on here.

But she was doing penance, she said. I wasn't convinced of that, either.

I turned sharply away and went into the kitchen to pour

another coffee. That was no way to conduct an investigation. I took my fresh cup to my desk. I'd piled all the books I had by Munro there. I took his biography of Galileo and browsed it. As I read, I began to turn pages angrily. No, Galileo was not a buffoonish sneak; Popes Urban the Eighth and Paul the Fifth were not ineffectual, backstabbing fops; Galileo's daughter was not a truck-driverish slut who posed as a nun; and Cardinal Bellarmine's mistress did not serve as a messenger between Bellarmine and Galileo. If Bellarmine had had a mistress, she wouldn't have been anything like Kimberly Eames.

I remembered something else about *Falling Bodies*. In what I'd seen of it before walking out, every character had gotten comic treatment, every character but the one played by Kimberly Eames. I'd watched her in three scenes: one with Dean Tolland as Bellarmine, one at a duke's party with Tolland again, and one with Player, when she was supposed to be delivering a warning to Galileo. Each of those scenes was exquisitely done, each was pulverizingly dramatic, and each of them riveted my attention, whetted my appetite for the next development—only to be followed by lunacy that made the most banal TV sitcom seem like one of Plato's Dialogues. To my knowledge, Eames had had no comic scenes in *Falling Bodies*.

So what had happened?

I slammed down my nearly empty mug, and Walker jumped from his lookout spot on the windowsill and ducked out of the room.

Since boyhood, I'd had a nearly uncontrollable hatred for the conscious desecration of the good. There was no valid reason on earth to practice it, not a single rationalization or justification for committing it. Watching *Falling Bodies*, I'd seen it once again, and I was old enough now to recognize the motives: malice, envy, fear . . . artlessly concealed by rationalizations that were complex and yet transparent. This film had desecrated its subject, Galileo, and its lead actress.

I cleaned up the mess on my desk, reassured Walker with a protracted neck massage. Then I sat back with a third coffee and looked through Munro's *A Matter of Record*, a collection of his essays, lectures and addresses. They were all about history and the philosophy of history. Most of the essays had appeared in scholarly journals over the years, some in general interest publications. My favorite was an extract of a paper he'd delivered to the Congress of Historians' Associations at Oxford University about ten years ago:

"Perhaps the best comparison between 'standard' history—the history most people encounter in school—and history imbued with life can be illustrated by using Howard Pyle's noted painting of the second charge up Bunker or Breed's Hill. It depicts a formation of British redcoats marching in flawless ranks up the hill beneath an undulating forest of upraised bayonets and muskets. The grenadiers must step over the bodies of comrades felled in the previous assault on the heights. All of the soldiers' and officers' faces are stoically fixed on the rebel entrenchments above them. One half of their ranks is in brilliant sunlight, the other half, closer to the viewer, is darkened by unseen clouds of cannon smoke. Altogether a powerful—but static—tableau, static if one did not sense that there is something else present in Pyle's composition that gives it life, lends it drama. One senses that this is more than just an accurate historical recreation of an event. One would be confounded by the sensory dilemma—unless and until one noticed the single grenadier in the last rank, his head turned surreptitiously, noting with apprehension the bodies of his comrades in the grass. That single face, and that singular expression, so subtly engineered by Pyle, brings drama to an otherwise lifeless recording of an historical event.

"This is what I seek to achieve in my own work, not to recreate the man out of the context of his times, but neither to deny the context the man, that is, to so bury him that he appears to be but a passive cipher in an impersonal event, or in a chain of events whose outcome we already know. History is not—should not be—an impersonal phenomenon, and ciphers do not make it, except when we allow them to. . . ."

Toward the end of that paper, Munro had written:

". . . *Mine is not a unique approach to writing history and communicating its value. It is, frankly, traditional, but traditional only because I believe it is the single proper and profitable approach. It is at sharp odds with current approaches which, generally, seek to present historical persons and events as either nuggets of predestination or snapshots of some school's dialectical process. The modern approach denies man one of his most unique assets—indeed, his sole defining and distinguishing asset—his volition. And it denies us our critical judgment and even our purpose; it robs an individual of all recognition, of credit, of discredit, of moral approbation, as the case may be. It reduces both subject and historian to the level of programmed ants.*

"Galileo was not fated to write The Starry Messenger; *nor was Bellarmine fated to straddle an ecclesiastical fence. Napoleon need not have decided to escape from Elba; and Gordon need not have elected to remain in Khartoum. Whatever the reasons and reasoning behind it, there is no single major or minor historical event that cannot be ascribed to a conscious decision by an individual. An event, after all, is simply an action. . . . The school that would elevate a single individual as an iconic chalice brimming with mysterious forces, and the school that would reduce him to a nearly insensate drone of a myriad of exocausative urgings, are but two sides of the same coin. I reject both."*

I slapped the book shut and set it on my desk. This was the same J. Forbes Munro who was supposed to have depicted, among other things, Galileo repeatedly dropping a couple of iron balls on the heads of two servants from the Leaning Tower of Pisa and establishing a scientific law according to whose "Ouch!" he heard first. The same J. Forbes Munro who, in his biography of Galileo, had caused a minor sensation by citing the research of a French scholar who had found documents that dismissed the apocryphal story once and for all. "It is not only slander that the dead cannot defend themselves against, but often legends and myths that may enhance their stature," wrote Munro in the biography. "Historians especially must bear in mind that this kind of fabrication can damage a reputation that may be sounder than that which the fabrication embellishes. It is perhaps harder to correct this kind of fabrication than it is to eradicate malicious hearsay."

J. Forbes Munro. Kimberly Eames. Patrick Player. Which name linked the other two? I could assume the two men knew each other, though Player had affected only a vague acquaintance with Munro's name. I'd already decided Player's conversation with me had been mostly a performance, with me serving as both audience and prompter. There were people who did that every day of their lives with their friends, enemies, and colleagues. Player was a professional at it. There was no way I could ever be certain when he was acting and when he wasn't. I wouldn't have cared if I didn't think he was hiding something about *Falling Bodies*.

I closed my eyes and made myself accept the possibility that I'd been given a performance by Kimberly Eames, too. "The most consummate, persuasive and stunning actress to come out of Hollywood in decades," declared one of the reviews on my desk. Said a drama magazine: "Virtuosity? Stamina? No one but Kimberly Eames has been able to pull off Benjamin Sharpe's curtain-raiser, *The Reunion*, a twenty-minute solo that requires an actress to portray five different women meeting ten years after college. Others have given commendable performances, but only Eames is able to convince you that there were five women on that stage. You were reminded of the fact of her presence only when the spotlight doused out the existence of her last character, and came on again, and there was Kimberly Eames, ready to receive the applause. And applause she would get, the kind that left one's palms stinging, the kind that made one wish it was still fashionable to throw bouquets of roses over the footlights."

I took my chilled coffee to the kitchen and dumped it into the sink.

On my way out through the lobby half an hour later, the doorman, Rob, said hello to my preoccupied nod, then added, "Oh, Mr. Hanrahan, thought you might want to know this." He jerked his head for me to come over to his desk. "There's that guy out there again."

"What guy?"

"When you went out yesterday morning, this guy who was hanging around went after you. He's there again."

"Point him out."

"He has a car he sits in, and sometimes he sits in the Silverado's plaza. Wearing a tan parka and golf cap now. Just ducked out for a coffee he brought back from Mac's Deli up the Avenue. He in the blue Volvo."

I went to the lobby's glass doors and pretended to check through my wallet. The Silverado was a newer apartment tower across Sixty-eighth from mine. There was a branch bank and a dry cleaner's on the ground floor, with a terraced, landscaped plaza on three sides of the building. The blue Volvo was parked on the Avenue. Someone was sitting on the passenger side, but I couldn't see his face, just a golf cap. If he was watching my lobby doors, it was through his rearview mirror. In the plaza, he could occupy one of the benches and watch through the elevated hedges. I ambled back to Rob. "You said since yesterday morning?"

"Yes, sir. You left your car parked outside the building Friday night, and when you went out to it Saturday morning, he got into his. I just happened to notice him again a while ago."

"Notice anyone else?'

Rob shook his head. "Not on my shift."

"Thanks, Rob. Let's see what happens. Be back later."

I stuck to my plan, which was to walk over to Fifth.

I put the possibility of a tail out of my mind until I entered the Doubleday bookstore on Fifth and Fifty-sixth. I minded my own business and fifteen minutes later had scooped up an armful of movie guides, movie industry histories, annotated reference books on all the stars and near-stars, past and present, and a book on the art of screenwriting.

Out of the corner of my eye I noticed another customer, a tall, sallow man a little older than me, in a tan parka and a checked golf cap, browsing through the remainder tables. I didn't look at him directly. He had dark eyes and an abbreviated moustache. He had a cold and sniffled a lot. I ignored him and took my books to a cash register.

In Barnes and Noble I checked my shopping bag at the counter, then went directly to the Entertainment section. It had many of the same titles I'd just bought, plus some others, including a collection of interviews with noted directors. I picked that one, then took the escalator down to the bargain basement. On the movie book table I leafed through a photo album, *Directions in American Cinema: The Last Fifty Years*. This one looked a lot like a number of others, a collection of movie stills with flimsy commentary. But one of the first stills featured Patrick Player as Jakin and Will Tucker as Lew, drummer and fife respectively, from *Drums of the Fore and Aft*. They stood together as they had near the climax of the picture, on a desolate plain littered with fallen British soldiers and abandoned rifles, knapsacks and helmets. Player looked about twelve years old, Tucker a little younger. Five minutes later in the story they would be dead, shot by Pathan tribesmen as they played "British Grenadiers" in an attempt to rally their cowardly regiment.

There was another still of Player, from much later in his career, as the sodden, slovenly ex-diplomat in *The Sargasso Sea*, wearing a three-day growth on his face and an inebriated leer. It was a handsome face that was trying to permanently sabotage itself. Both stills were paired on the same page and shared the same caption: "From the hoary chutzpa of yesteryear, drunk on a vision that was recklessly grandiose and heedlessly extravagant, to a vision that experimented with the maturity of disillusionment and soul-splitting candor, Patrick Player's film career has followed—if not in fact influenced—the course of

American filmmaking for almost four decades. Top: Army bandsmen Player and Tucker bravely face hostile Afghan marksmen. Bottom: Player faces hostile glare of consular official Elliott Rhodes, proving that the flora wasn't the only lushness in steamy Central America." Only half of Rhodes's face was in the frame. Something tickled my memory about him, too. I bought the album. I wanted those stills.

Golf Cap hadn't followed me inside the store. He was loitering outside near a pretzel vendor on the corner.

I crossed Fifth Avenue and walked up to Nat Sherman's Tobacconist to the World. There I bought two cartons of the house brand for evenings at home and one for Rob the doorman. I stopped on the corner of Fifty-fourth to listen to a guitarist playing for change. He was good. After twenty minutes, I dropped a five into his guitar case and worked my way through the crowd with my shopping bag. I glanced back and saw Golf Cap drop a bill into the guitar case, too.

I turned west on Fifty-third and headed for the Museum of Modern Art. I had no use for the place as far as its "art" was concerned, but it had a fairly large shop with a wide range of movie books. But it was closed to the public today; a sign on the door read "Private Party." Well, I'd try tomorrow.

I stopped to light a cigarette, and my glance fell on the artwork over the entrance of a new office building across the street. I'd seen it before and it had left me baffled. Now it began to make some sense, and that wasn't necessarily a compliment. It was a trio of statues, in a very dark brown patina, of expertly detailed monks' robes in various stages of supplication. The action of the robes led one's eye to the subject, but when the eye got there, there was nothing to see. No limbs emerged from the billowing sleeves, no sandaled feet peeked out from under the hems, and no faces peered out from under the cowls. There was only emptiness. I stood there a while and studied the group, certain that I was close to a connection between it and modern pictures and the other fields of art today that left me puzzled, indifferent and angry at the same time. There was style here, and a conclusion, but what was it?

I frowned, then picked up my shopping bag and headed back home. Golf Cap was in a knot of Sunday strollers passing by the Museum.

Back in my lobby, I handed Rob one of the Nat Sherman cartons. "Thanks for the tip," I said. "I'd never have noticed him otherwise."

Rob took the carton and put it under the desk counter. "You on a case, Mr. Hanrahan?"

"No, but *he* obviously is."

"I almost called the cops," said Rob. "Guys who hang around outside like that are usually up to no good. But I thought you might want to know about him first."

"Let me know if you see his partner. If I'm under a twenty-four hour watch, he's got to have help."

Back in my apartment, I removed the books from the bag and put them on my desk, then went to the picture window and looked down the thirty stories. There he was again, crossing Sixty-eighth with a white bag, heading for his Volvo. He'd gone to Mac's Deli for another coffee, I guessed. I watched for a few minutes. The Volvo didn't move. It had begun raining again.

Chapter 9

I didn't think Mrs. Sismond of San Francisco was responsible for Golf Cap. Any private investigator she might have approached would have told her that watching me wouldn't necessarily lead to her son. Or any honest one. And I doubted she was pursuing her son anyway. Harry Sismond's note, describing her as a "manipulative, domineering bitch who probably drove Dad to an early grave," should have bought him the distance he wanted. He'd had to consult my dictionary a number of times while composing the message.

So it must have been either Kimberly Eames or Patrick Player. There were no loose ends dangling from any of my other recent cases. Neither Carol Holvick, the book editor, nor Albert Lundy, the lit agent, had seemed overly curious about my interest in J. Forbes Munro, but one of them had warned Eames, and either of them might have warned Player. To get surveillance on me, either Eames or Player had moved fast.

I eliminated John Tigrini, attorney, as having sounded the

alarm because I hadn't even been given the chance to explain myself to him or to anyone else in his law firm.

I didn't mind being watched. I could tolerate it up to a point. . . .

Eames or Player. Or Eames *and* Player. I preferred to think Player had hired someone to tag me. His memory was too convenient—forgetful of Munro and an unnamed collaborator, retentive of the name of a private eye he'd seen mentioned in a newspaper months ago. It was more plausible that someone had told Player about me Friday evening or Saturday, someone to whom my name might have been vaguely familiar and who had done quick research of his own.

It was what I wanted to believe. My few moments with Kimberly Eames had brought a sense of rapport. I didn't want to believe she had been acting.

I looked at it coldly. Eames or Player. Or Eames *and* Player. What their common interest might be I couldn't guess.

She was doing penance. Or so she had said. How long had she been doing it? Five years? Or six months? From the day she'd married Munro, or since his death? And what was her definition of penance? Was it Elaine Card's brand? Patrick Player's? And penance for what?

No woman who looked, spoke and behaved like Kimberly Eames had any business doing penance.

"...He was a prisoner of the idea that the institution for which he held great respect, the institution which he viewed as a valuer and promulgator of truth, could neither contemplate nor commit wrong. Some allege that Galileo was vainglorious enough to think that he could win it over to his position and thus not only advance truth but also protect himself from the wrath of certain individuals who could use the Church as an instrument of power and an enforcer of ignorance. I would not call him so much vainglorious as tragically naïve. It was not that he overestimated his own person, mind and reputation; rather, it was that he placed his trust, quite against his intent, in those whom he *regarded as being at least as sturdy and unfrightened in mind as he regarded himself. Some of these men had openly admired and encouraged him, so long as the dogma they represented and were bound to defend was not fundamentally threatened by the truth. Others were suspicious of Galileo from the beginning of his public life, and viewed him as the antithesis of the ageless thinker, who, in their eyes, should harbor within himself an unquestioning devotion to received wisdom and an obsequious deference to established authority. But I do not believe that Galileo was as astute an observer of human character as he was of the stars and planets, or he might have formulated early in his life the conditional law which proposes that shamed and timid friends are usually worse enemies than one's dedicated opponents...."*

I closed Munro's *Galileo* and set it aside, then swiveled my chair to face the overcast day beyond my office window. It had rained off and on. I could see a few people in office buildings near my own, standing patiently at their windows, apparently hoping for the weather to clear.

I had searched out that passage in Galileo late last night. Browsing through movie books, I'd gotten a vague notion. It gained a little shape as I reviewed Player's film career. After a certain point, his career was disgraceful. His next picture after *Drums of the Fore and Aft* was *Incident at Rowdy River*, released two years later. As I remembered, it had been a western about hero worship, though according to two of the books I'd bought, its theme was either "role modeling" or "male bonding with misogynic overtones." Patrick Player had played the boy, the late Dean Tolland the sheriff of Rowdy River, Montana, and Donald Pierce the boy's father. Tolland tracked a vicious outlaw as far as Player's father's ranch, in pursuit of the man who'd murdered a mining family three years earlier. Player's father was that very same outlaw, who'd bought a prosperous ranch with stolen gold and then sent for his wife and son who were living in St. Louis. Player, as an adolescent, had to choose between accepting Tolland's evidence that his father was a fraud and a murderer, and the ostensive upright character of his father.

After *Rowdy River* came *Swift Sword*, set during the English Civil War. Player, in his first starring role, portrayed a renegade hero who fought both the Royalists and the Roundheads. It was an intriguing, bold idea about a disinherited baron who cursed both sides. I remembered it, too. It was my favorite "swashbuckler." It had run for years on late night television, then abruptly vanished.

The rights to it had been bought by producers Leonard Sproul and Albert Grunnian, of Twin Dolphins Productions, to prepare for a remake starring Player again, but as a Royalist officer, and his son, Brett Player, as the young hero. This had happened about fifteen years after the original was released. From the synopses of the remake in two of my books, I saw that it was shot as a farce, with sight gags, pratfalls, lewd scenes, pointless swordplay, and horse manure jokes. The public hadn't found it so funny, and it flopped.

Brett Player, noted one of the books, had died in a car accident a month after the picture had been finished.

Patrick Player's career had been headed down long before that tragedy. Player had appeared in a succession of controversial duds and barely noticed bombs. I read through the titles, and nothing caught my eye. He'd done TV guest spots and game shows.

Then, about nine years ago, he'd started a comeback in *The Plaster Men*, about intrigue in Washington, then *God's Fool*, which traced the life of Henry the First's jester, and *The Sargasso Sea*, which Player had also directed. The *Swift Sword* remake, *Falling Bodies* and other films had followed.

Onward and upward with the career.

It fit well with Hollywood, which was going the other way.

I rose from my chair, pulled the blinds up as far as they would go, and stood at the window.

What had brought about Player's decline? Actors, like other

people, could be embarrassingly stupid about the meaning of what they did. Some grew contemptuous of their field and didn't care how they were used. But I couldn't believe either explanation applied to Player. He had to care about what he was doing. How could he exert so much effort in a third-rate piece of crap like *Trackside* and not care?

A better question might be: How could he care so much about devoting his talent to a piece of crap?

He hadn't denied my appraisal of *Trackside*. Instead, he'd given me a sincere-sounding apologia about the dearth of appreciative audiences. I'd heard actors blame their absence from the scene on a scarcity of worthwhile scripts. That I could understand, depending on what they called worthwhile. Player, however, was the only actor I'd heard blame the public. Yet audiences didn't set the terms in the arts, they were led. Player seemed intelligent enough to know that.

I took a break, dealt with the mail: three bills, two checks and two queries. At eleven-thirty a messenger in a wet blue poncho arrived with Patrick Player's invitation to his post-banquet party on Wednesday. I signed for it, and opened the envelope. The card read: "Admit Two on My Personal Invitation" in gold script, and was signed with a flourish by the actor. I slid it back inside the envelope and dropped it inside my open briefcase on the floor. I went to pencil in the occasion on my desk calendar, and saw that I hadn't flipped the pages. I saw a note to myself to call Harry Sismond with his mother's response, which I'd done. It was November now.

My mind idled.

Then I suddenly knew I was right about who had called Kimberly Eames and Patrick Player. Or at least I was ninety-nine percent certain: Carol Holvick, Munro's editor, had dimed me. Ellen Romero, in her gossip column, had made a remark about people not being able to refuse me answers to my questions. In the same column she had quoted me as saying personal curiosity produced a lot of my cases. Kimberly Eames had repeated the first part on Saturday morning. Player had mentioned the second Saturday night backstage. Holvick was the only person I'd spoken to in the beginning who recognized my name.

I picked up my phone, called Ellen Romero at the *Chronicle*. Her secretary put me on hold while she asked Romero whether or not she was in, and the next voice I heard was the columnist's. "Mr. Hanrahan, hello. To what do I owe this honor?"

I said, "My personal curiosity. Are you too busy to talk?"

"Actually, no, not right now. We've just put the paper to bed. I covered the United Nations Halloween Party for Children last night. It's a scream."

"You associate with the nicest people," I said. "What was their theme this year? 'Terrorism or Treat'?"

"Now, now, Chess, that's no way to be. Think of all the poor, starving people around the world they're helping. How can you doubt their intentions?"

"I can because those very same people are still poor and starving after sixty years of help. But that's not why I called."

"What can I do for you?"

"Tell me—did someone call you recently about me?"

"About you?"

"As I was portrayed in your column last July. You remember the Beekman Tower party?"

"That's right. Someone did call about that. She was there, too, it seems. Carol Holvick. She remembered my column, couldn't remember when it ran. She was *very* interested in you, Chess. Too interested for words."

I chuckled. "I don't think it was that personal. Listen, I'm onto something rich. When it's ready, I'll give you first crack."

"How rich?" asked the columnist.

"Hollywood."

Romero laughed. "Any bodies?"

"No, not this time."

"Are you on a case?"

"No, but I've met the most interesting people lately."

"Give me a hint."

"No, I can't, because I'm not entirely certain myself what's going on."

"Oh, you wouldn't know what's going on until someone tried to autograph your body with an Uzi. Well, I've got to go. Would you believe I'm on my way to meet Elaine Card? She's giving a press conference luncheon for society columnists and other truth-seekers in her penthouse on the East River. I think she wants to bribe us into saying nice things about her mental illness soiree this Wednesday. And to think that just six years ago she was selling arts and crafts pottery for the poor at Earth Love festivals and collecting alimony from her ex-husband, a trucker whose rig she also collected in the settlement."

There was no reason now to see Carol Holvick. I could understand her trying to protect the privacy of an author's widow. But why also inform Player?

The chimes of the Metropolitan Tower clock reminded me it was noon. Romero's mention of lunch reminded me I was hungry. It was drizzling outside but I wouldn't mind. I put my suit coat on, then my overcoat, and as I was reaching for my lighter and cigarette case, someone knocked on my door. I said come in.

And she did. Kimberly Eames.

Chapter 10

She wore a dark blue raincoat, dress boots, a scarf, and a trilby-like riding hat, both brims down. And sunglasses. Only the sunglasses were incongruous. She took them off, smiled apologetically. "Were you going out, Mr. Hanrahan?"

"Only to lunch," I said. "Would you like to join me?"

She fingered the sunglasses in her hand. "I don't know. I haven't been to a restaurant in Manhattan for so long. . . ."

"We can walk, or order out. Or take a cab to Brooklyn Heights."

"I don't want to put you to any trouble."

"It's too late to hope that, Mrs. Munro. A little more won't matter." I reached for the phone and dialed Paulette's, a little place just three blocks up on Park Avenue. It was quiet, with a fair menu and discreet booths. I went there sometimes to be alone. I spoke with the maître 'd. There would be a table at twelve-thirty.

While I was on the phone, Kimberly Eames roamed around

the office. She ran a finger over the tops of my eclectic collection of law and reference books, glanced at the case souvenirs behind glass in the cabinet, and studied the Raphael and Schreyvogel prints. She spent the longest time in front of my brass motto, staring at it for a moment longer than it had taken her to read it. She turned to me when I replaced the receiver.

"There's a place not far from here, a five minute walk." I said. "If we leave now, we can go right to our table."

She looked anxious, so I added, "It's a pricey establishment, but people don't go there to show themselves off."

"Thank you."

"I know you weren't just in the neighborhood. What can I do for you?"

"I should have called first. You might not have been in."

"I almost wasn't."

"Why do you pair those two?" Kimberly Eames asked, glancing again at the prints facing each other on opposite walls. "They're so dissimilar in subject, yet somehow they go together."

"Even Chances" depicted an Indian and a cavalryman reining in their mounts from a gallop, tomahawk and saber raised to deal the other a fatal blow. The central figures in the "School of Athens" were Plato and Aristotle, striding together through a great thinker-crowded hall, one man gesturing upward to heaven, the other extending a hand palm-down over the earth.

"One conflict is a form of the other," I said, glad that she'd expressed curiosity. "Most of my cases fall somewhere in between—thematically speaking."

"Where would you place the one you're investigating now?"

"I can't say yet."

"Why not?"

"I'm not on what I'd call a case."

It was still drizzling, but not hard enough for us to hail a cab. Kimberly Eames dropped her sunglasses inside her shoulder bag and drew out a collapsible umbrella, which she snapped open. I offered my arm, and she hooked a hand on it, almost shyly. As we started, I said, "How did you get here?"

"I took a cab from the Gardens."

"Do you have a car?"

"Yes, but I don't use it much in the city."

"Well," I said as we crossed Thirty-fourth Street, "what *can* I do for you?"

"Nothing," she said. "That is, I'd like you to stop investigating my late husband."

"I'm not investigating him."

"You're trying to determine the authorship of that screenplay, Mr. Hanrahan. You said so yourself."

"That's not investigating your late husband."

"From my standpoint, it is."

"What *is* your standpoint, Mrs. Munro?"

"That anything ever said, written or observed by Forbes, has to do with him."

"If he didn't write that screenplay, then your standpoint can't include him."

"I don't know who did write it, and I don't much care to learn. But I know for a fact that Forbes had nothing to do with it."

"Even though he's credited with it?"

"Even so."

I shrugged. "If he wasn't responsible, then I want to know who was, and why." I studied her profile, and beat down a desire to run a hand over it.

"Why won't you take my word for it?" she asked.

I hustled us across Thirty-fifth. "The contradiction is just the tickler, Mrs. Munro. If your late husband didn't write that screenplay, then obviously someone did who didn't get credit for it. Surely that's occurred to you."

"It has."

"Now, I happen to know that those credits are not only guaranteed by contract between a screenwriter and the production company but also by a screenwriter's union contract. My point is that whoever *did* write that screenplay waived a clause in his personal contract, and his union never got wind of it."

"A very astute observation," said Kimberly Eames.

"Thank you. Considering the power the unions wield in that industry, it's a curious state of affairs, don't you think? You were a part of the business. You should know better than I."

"Yes."

"So, given all that, don't you think it odd? Members of a craft union could threaten a job action in a dispute over a gaffer's credit. Yet the true author of this screenplay—for a film that's been called a minor American classic—forgoes all credit and acclaim."

"I . . . never doubted the oddity, Mr. Hanrahan."

"Yet *you* don't much care to learn who waived the credit."

"I'm sorry you feel that way," she said. "I can't help you."

"Why not?"

"Because, I'm afraid . . . I'm afraid that knowing wouldn't make a difference."

"It would make a difference to me," I said. "That's why I'm doing this. And when I learn who was the true author of that screenplay, I'm going to try to see to it that he gets public credit. He may not thank me, considering the nature of the screenplay."

"Are . . . you closer to learning?"

"No closer than I am to you, Mrs. Munro."

"How do you mean?"

"I mean that I also want to know what has paralyzed you so that you don't care that your husband's name has been sullied. In that sense, I'm not close to you."

A faint smiled bent Kimberly Eames's mouth. "Is that how you plan to spend our lunch together—by interrogating me?"

"More or less."

"I believe you're enjoying yourself, Mr. Hanrahan."

"Of course."

Dmitri, the headwaiter, greeted us in the foyer after we'd

checked our coats and whisked us straight to our booth. Kimberly Eames glanced around at the decor and seemed to relax when she saw that no one was staring at us. We ordered vodka gimlets and read our menus. We were in an Italian mood. I ordered the veal alla Milanese, she the gnocchi alla Romana. The soft light added an extra shade of red to her hair and a luster to her pearl earrings. She wore a fine tweed jacket over a white silk blouse. When she moved her hands—pianist's hands, I thought, long and deceptively fragile-looking—the light played on the diamonds of her wedding ring.

"Was your husband ever a member of the Guild?"

"No."

"Was he ever paid for the screenplay?"

"Yes. He received checks—enormous checks—regularly. I still get them. But none of them has ever been cashed, or ever will be."

"Why not?"

"Because he did not write that screenplay."

"It's been five years since *Falling Bodies* was released. What's happened to all those checks?"

"Forbes sent them back to the studio—Twin Dolphins—with letters stating that an error had been made. But his letters were never acknowledged. The checks continued to come. He tore them up. I still do."

I leaned closer to her over the tablecloth. "Mrs. Munro, every time you answer one of my questions, I get more curious. You can't blame me. Think of what I've told you—and what you haven't denied. Think of what you'd told me—and what I haven't doubted."

"It doesn't make any sense, does it?" she replied.

"No, it doesn't." I took a sip of my gimlet. "Unless I'm greatly mistaken, we agree in our evaluation of *Falling Bodies*. At least you haven't defended it. Munro's name is associated with that rubbish. By itself, I think that's a crime. If he truly had nothing to do with it, that's something worse. I'd like to see his name publicly dissociated from that picture."

"Why does that matter so much to you, Mr. Hanrahan?"

"Because there isn't much left for me to enjoy today, except what's rooted in the past. Art, music, drama, pictures. I want to hang on to what little I do enjoy. Your late husband's work is one of those things. I'd like to preserve his reputation, publicly and in my own mind." I paused. "Of course, I might be mistaken about him. Perhaps he *did* write that screenplay. If he did, then someone else wrote all his books and essays and ghostwrote his lectures. Which poses the same scale of contradiction."

"It would," she said. She seemed to change the subject. "What do you think the things you don't enjoy are rooted in?"

I thought of the sculptures of empty robes and shook my head.

"I think I know," she said. "It's deliberate . . . destruction of everything I used to think art was about: dignity, grace, goodness. What drives that?"

I let her tell me.

"It's malice, Mr. Hanrahan. I know quite a lot about malice. It destroyed my career."

"Whose?"

She ignored the question. "It starts with a sense of injustice, doesn't it? But if you're helpless to do anything about it, the feeling grows and gnaws at your insides until all you can feel is hate . . . and helplessness. And you never meant to feel that way about anything, ever."

"It can do that," I conceded. "Whose malice destroyed your career?"

Kimberly Eames seemed to rouse herself and shook her head. "No. We won't talk about that. Please?"

Before I could object, the waiter came with our appetizers. I was glad he had. It gave me time to reconsider pressing her on the matter. One obstacle at a time, I told myself. Remember: she came to you. You've awakened something. Let her get used to you.

"Would you excuse me for a moment, Mr. Hanrahan?" she

asked, rising. I thought I saw tears in her eyes, as she smiled and turned away from me.

I sat and picked at the pear salad. Five minutes later Dmitri approached the table with a hard, trance-like expression that meant he was embarrassed. He bent down to say softly, "The lady asked me to tell you that she is sorry and apologizes for the inconvenience. She asked me to give you this." He laid a crisp fifty-dollar bill on the tablecloth. "I've already told the chef to cancel her order."

"Thanks, Dmitri," I said, picking up the bill and turning it over, half expecting to find a note of explanation on the other side. Dmitri turned and went back to his duties.

I ate alone.

Chapter 11

There would have been no point in going after her. She could have flagged a cab and been several traffic lights away before I reached the restaurant door. I tucked the fifty dollars inside my jacket. I wasn't surprised, but I worried that if she had come to me for reassurance, then I'd only assured her that I was a source of pain.

I didn't think she sought me out only to ask me to stop my investigation. That could have been done in a note, which would have saved her the discomfort of venturing out. She had come because she had wanted to see me.

I tried to imagine the magnitude of wrong she had suffered. The question began to compete with my interest in the true authorship of the *Falling Bodies* screenplay. The two were closely linked. Twin Dolphins Productions must be keeping an odd set of books for that picture, as checks were returned or torn up.

My coffee grew cold as I brooded over the questions I never got to ask her.

●

Ploughsmith College lay in a suburban purgatory that was neither city borough nor Long Island county. It was surrounded by a tawdry neighborhood, the campus a handful of old brick buildings with some newer glass and concrete ones that were aging badly. There were tired-looking trees, inexpertly pruned hedges, brown lawns. The walkways winding through it all had their own potholes and sinking slabs. Altogether, a dismal place in which to seek knowledge and invest in one's future. I parked my car in the visitors' lot near the glum Administration building.

A frumpy-looking dean's secretary, whose ID tag said Cynthia Vogel, was more cooperative than I had expected her to be. I introduced myself over the counter, and asked for the name of someone who had been a colleague of J. Forbes Munro. She asked me why. I said I had some questions about his books. After some obligatory commiseration about Munro's death, followed by obligatory commentary on the city's crime problem, she said, "Well, you might want to talk with Professor Downey in History Studies. They were very good friends." She turned to consult a chart tacked to a plaster wall near her desk. "He's in class now, but he should be in his office about three-thirty."

"Where is his office?"

"In Beal Hall." She gave me directions. Then she paused. "Are you a policeman?"

"No," I answered.

"You look like one," she said. "I mean, you look like you ought to be one."

"Why do you say that?"

"My late husband was a policeman. You have honest eyes, like his." She smiled, brought herself back to business. "If you go now, you can get to Beal Hall in a few minutes. Sometimes Professor Downey lets his classes out early."

Professor Downey taught American and European history and had occupied his tiny, book-crammed office in the basement of Beal Hall for over ten years. He was short, stocky, about fifty-five, with a red, wind-burned face, gray hair and a neatly trimmed silver beard. He reminded me of a sea captain; that impression was helped by a couple of photos on the wall of him and presumably his wife aboard a small sailing boat. He accepted my interest in Munro, but when I got down to specifics—*Falling Bodies*—he said, "You might want to ask his wife about that."

"I've tried. She's reluctant to talk about it."

"Then I'm afraid I can't," said Downey with a regretful but resolute smile. "You see, Forbes was a dear friend of mine. If his widow won't speak about it, then I can't allow myself to." He shrugged. "Not that I'd be able to enlighten you on the matter. Both Forbes and his wife were quite reticent about it."

"So are quite a few other people. Well, I had lunch with Mrs. Munro a little over an hour ago in Manhattan. I mean, with Kimberly Eames."

"Ah," Downey chuckled. "My wife and I haven't seen her since Forbes's funeral. We've invited her over to dinner, invited her out, and even tried to talk ourselves over to her place. But she's simply severed all social contact that we're aware of." He sighed. "We're the only two people here at Ploughsmith who know who she is, or was. We've not talked about her or the *Falling Bodies* matter with anyone. She never came to the school, never met anyone else here. The Dean of the college and the department head were a little put off by Munro's refusal to introduce her, but there was little they could do about it."

"Tell me something about him."

"About Forbes? What exactly would you like to know?"

"Aside from his being credited with that screenplay—well, your own thoughts about him."

"Margaret—that's my wife—Margaret and I were surprised at the differences between Forbes and Kimberly, between their years and their backgrounds, but we needn't have worried. Kimberly was mature beyond her years, aside from having an exceptional head on her lovely shoulders and a sound education. She was solid. I imagine she matured at a very early age or during her climb in Hollywood."

I shook my head. "No, not in Hollywood. Tell me: Were you surprised when you learned that Munro had written that screenplay?"

"Yes. We all were. That was about five years ago, wasn't it? I didn't learn of it until Bill—William Harker, our ancient history instructor—came in one Monday morning and said he'd taken his kids over the weekend to see *Falling Bodies* and wished he hadn't. But he'd noticed the name of the screenwriter. And then everyone knew."

"What was Munro's explanation?"

"That it was a coincidence of similar names. We didn't believe him, he knew it, and but no one pressed him on the issue. We secretly kept an eye out for a new wardrobe or a sports car in the faculty lot or even a retirement announcement from Forbes. None of that happened. And of course everyone in the department went to see *Falling Bodies*—and also wished we hadn't."

"What did you think then?"

Downey frowned. "On one hand the film violated my knowledge of Forbes's character. It was as inconceivable that he'd belittle Galileo, or even his enemies, as that he'd write a glamorizing biography of Hitler. On the other hand, it was the treatment of Galileo that struck me, at least, as typical Forbes Munro. Not the comedy or the bawdy episodes, but the plain, unembellished angle on Galileo. That, and little pieces of information that Forbes had included in his biography which I believe no other screenwriter could have known enough to include in the story." Downey raised a finger. "My own personal hypothesis is that the people who made the film bought the rights to Forbes's books and had someone else write the screenplay. Forbes made a bad decision and went along with it. And regretted it, which would explain his silence. Though if that were the case, we'd have seen a different credit, something like 'Screenplay by Mel deHack, based on the book by J. Forbes Munro,' instead of 'Screenplay by J. Forbes Munro.'

I asked Forbes about that. He denied having anything to do with it. We never discussed it again."

"Why not?"

"Well, first, because he didn't want to discuss it. So I curbed my curiosity. It was about six months after that film came out that he asked me to be best man at his wedding. Surprise again! I'd not one hint that he was even seeing anyone. It was a private ceremony in Pennsylvania. He asked me to swear to secrecy about it, which I did, or rather Margaret and I did. We were the only guests. There weren't any headlines about it, to my knowledge, but then I don't follow celebrity news or the society pages. As couples, we exchanged occasional visits. But something had happened between us. I've never been able to put my finger on it. Forbes went on as usual here at Ploughsmith, and even finished his last book."

"On Vivaldi," I said.

"That, and his course load here, AHS meetings, speaking engagements, faculty business, and so on. Nothing changed. I got the impression that he was working on a new book. He never talked about it. If he had a project, he never got to finish it, and only Kimberly and his publisher and her lawyers know for sure."

"I'll ask her about it."

Downey went on about how J. Forbes Munro left a prestigious university in Maine to come to Ploughsmith. "He helped put this school on the academic map, Mr. Hanrahan. The administration gave him carte blanche to teach whatever he wanted and publish whatever he wrote. That's why he came here. Well, it's been over fifteen years, and I think we've assembled as fine a faculty in the humanities as can be found anywhere in a school this size."

"Can you fill me in on his et ceteras—his parents, schooling, his life before Ploughsmith?"

"I could," said Downey, "though I can't imagine how any of that could have anything to do with your interest in the screenplay."

I cocked my head. "I didn't know him personally. I'd like to have. I have access to the public highlights of his life, and that's all. I'd like a better picture of him. I subscribe to his idea of biography. I want to neither deny him the context of his times, nor the context the man."

"Forbes would have appreciated you as a fan," Downey said.

"He would have appreciated a little justice to his reputation, too."

"Well, since you put it that way," smiled the professor, "a brief biographical sketch of J. Forbes Munro. He had an ideal childhood, apparently, sponsored by ideal parents. His father was an aeronautical design engineer in Seattle, his mother was an accomplished amateur pianist. They did well enough to send Forbes to some top notch private schools. Why, he even went to the same prep school I did, Vickers Prep, up near Boston. He was a freshman a year after I'd graduated. Let me see, he went to Graham College in Charlotte, did a few years' graduate work at Dalhousie in Maine, then he won a Burroughs scholarship to Oxford. That was where he discovered the Larkspur-Macaulay forgeries—"

"The what?"

Downey grinned impishly, and narrated the story of how Munro had made his reputation as a scholar. Apparently another American historian by the name of Marston Larkspur had found an essay on Edmund Burke by Thomas Macaulay. In the stacks of the British Museum, Munro found a note from Macaulay to some Scottish historian saying that he had burned the essay in disgust. Larkspur's discovery was examined and discovered to be a forgery, one painstakingly created by Larkspur himself. Discovery of the forgery invalidated a number of book-length papers that had been based on Larkspur's "find."

"Was that a big news story?"

Downey shook his head. "Storm in a teacup. I mean, it was big news for historians and academia. Larkspur was discredited and died about a year after the very young Forbes made his discovery of Macaulay's letter, which was authenticated. Forbes had no problem finding a faculty position when he returned to the States."

"Did he ever make news again?"

"Not the same way," said Downey. "He got involved in the usual controversies and disputes—as we all do—but they don't matter. He was forever at war with the New History and the Neo-New History. He wrote more essays and articles than the rest of us in this department put together." He fell silent. "There was one dispute. . . . It was out of the ordinary for Forbes. It wasn't about history or research methods."

"What was it about?"

"It had to do with the remaking of an older film. I still don't understand why he bothered himself with it, or even why it bothered him so much. Either he objected to the film or he objected to somebody's review of it, I can't remember which. He wrote a long letter to the *Times,* which was printed and touched off a public debate about the film or the review, or both." Downey threw his hands wide. "And I can't recall the picture's name."

I smiled a little *"Swift Sword?"*

"That's it!" exclaimed the professor. "An exchange of letters went on for about a month in the *Times.* Then Forbes was invited by the *New Observer* to contribute a full-length article on the topic, which appeared a few months later. Does it matter?"

I sat for a moment with my own thoughts. There had been a five-year gap between the remake of *Swift Sword* and the appearance of *Falling Bodies,* both of which had starred Patrick Player. I glanced at my watch. It was nearly quarter to five. I said, "Thanks for letting me eat up your time like this, Professor Downey. I think that'll hold me for a while."

Downey waved a hand. "No problem. Is that your only interest in Forbes? You don't think he wrote that screenplay?"

"No, I don't think he did."

"I wish you luck. Especially in dealing with Kimberly. How is she?"

"She's fine. She just needs a little nudge, that's all." I took out my wallet. "Here's my card. If you can think of anything else, could you give me a call?"

In the visitors' lot, I stopped to light a cigarette before getting into my car. It gave me a chance to eye the blue Volvo sitting in a slot on the other side of the section. There was someone in it, but it didn't look like Golf Cap. I fought an impulse to knock on the glass and introduce myself. Instead I unlocked my car door and got in. I started my engine, then switched off. The blue Volvo started up a second later. Subtle. I switched on again, backed out, and forgot the Volvo.

On the main street a quarter mile from the college, I spotted a florist's shop. I stopped long enough to go in and arrange to have a half-dozen roses sent to Cynthia Vogel, secretary to the dean at Ploughsmith. On a blank card I wrote, "Thanks for your help. Here's something for *your* eyes. Chess Hanrahan." Then I put it in an envelope, sealed it, and picked out a blue glass vase for the roses.

Chapter 12

Traffic was bad into and out of
Manhattan, so it was almost seven o'clock before I reached my
office, and nearly seven-thirty before I found a parking space,
three blocks away. I went up, collected things I wanted from
my desk, checked the answering machine.

Kimberly Eames had called. "Mr. Hanrahan, I apologize for
my behavior this afternoon. I . . . don't know when I'll be able to
see you again. Please forgive me."

Of course I'd forgive her.

The urge to drive out to Forest Hills Gardens was almost
irresistible.

Instead I loaded my briefcase and headed home.

On my way to the car, I passed a liquor store and was ten
steps past its window when something registered in my mind
and drew me back. In a corner of the window display was an
advertising prop, a cardboard cut-out of a Magellan
Champagne ad. It was at least ten years old, the sunset colors

faded. Kimberly Eames stood on a balcony in an evening dress, gazing out over the buildings around her, her folded hands holding a long-stemmed glass of champagne. Discreetly printed at the bottom of the ad were the words, "*At the end of a journey . . . Magellan. . . .*"

She was nameless then, also appearing in a commercial for a men's cologne.

I went into the store. Arguing with the store clerk, I pulled out the fifty-dollar bill that Kimberly Eames left for me in the restaurant. The clerk took the ad from the window, blew dust off it, and handed it over in exchange for the fifty. I opened my briefcase and dropped the ad into it.

At home, I found a place for it on my desk. Walker jumped up and padded over the books and papers to inspect it. I said to him, "You'd better hope she's not allergic to cats, Mister."

I woke early Tuesday, reviewed the previous evening's work. I had downloaded a list of Patrick Player's pictures, then a list of my old movie idol Elliott Rhodes's. Their careers had followed similar courses: spectacular beginnings, disappointing declines, and steady comebacks. In the comeback phase they had appeared together in three films: *The Sargasso Sea, The Plaster Men,* and the remake of *Swift Sword.* Kimberly Eames had worked with both men, first with Rhodes in *Fraction of Fear,* then with Player in *Falling Bodies.* I didn't know why I was looking for a connection among the three of them. That certainly wasn't much of one.

But I had put together a timeline that clarified the overlapping histories.

There was a five-year gap between the release of the *Swift Sword* remake and *Falling Bodies.* Five years, that is, between the picture Munro had written a letter and an article about and the picture for which he'd received a screenplay credit. Shortly after *Falling Bodies,* Munro and Kimberly Eames had married. Five years after *Falling Bodies,* Munro had been killed, earlier this year.

As far as I could find, Rhodes hadn't appeared in any film since *Fraction of Fear*. That one had come out about six months before *Falling Bodies*.

Rhodes's career had begun on television. I remembered each of his series, which came as I was growing up. It hadn't been so much the characters he played that I found interesting as the character he brought to his roles. His leitmotif had always been studied reticence, then action. His face that could give life to the driest dialogue.

I smiled at my recollection that I had probably copied Rhodes's facial mannerisms in my early teens. He had played an aloof cowhand for several years in *Trails West*, a dogged homicide detective in *Hazzard's City*, and a mix of dramatic and comedic roles in *P.M. Theater*, some episodes of which he had written or directed.

His last series, Chimera Jones, was the one he was most famous for. He portrayed the title character, a suave, dapper secret agent, who became so popular that Rhodes's opening credits silhouette was licensed for men's cologne and for ads for casual wear. An early movie, *Conspiracy in Crystal*, I remembered vividly as probably the best espionage picture I'd ever seen; Rhodes had starred as a double agent against the Soviets and had been nominated for an Academy Award. Several more heroic films followed, then for several years nothing, then a comeback—like Player's—built on roles mocking his former image. He had costarred with comedian Bucky Bruno in *Slap Leather*, a commercially successful parody of Westerns. The comedies had been followed by parts in low-budget horror movies and other B-pictures. And a part with Player in *The Plaster Men*.

Player and Rhodes had overlapped in earlier days, too. I got another cup of coffee and read on. Both men had attended the Royal Academy of Drama in London in their teens. Player had been a regular student, Rhodes on a scholarship. Player was the last in the line of a notable theater family; Rhodes had grown up in Minnesota and his father had been an insurance claims adjuster. The same studio, Twin Dolphins, had financed two of Player's early pictures—*Rowdy River* and *Swift Sword.* Malcolm Player, Patrick's director-father, had controlled distribution rights, which on his death were willed to his son.

I pressed on, jumping back and forth between the two actors. Rhodes had created the Chimera Jones character and had written many of the series' scripts. Player had formed his own production company, Autumn Harvest. The company had put up the money for *The Sargasso Sea* and *God's Fool.* Rhodes had tried a similar strategy and ended up in financial trouble. He worked at union scale to help repay Twin Dolphins for its investment in two projects. His last film had been with Kimberly Eames in *Fraction of Fear* five years ago.

Player was in command of his career, I thought. Rhodes was not.

By ten o'clock I'd done my morning chores, had gathered all my notes into the briefcase, and was out the door. By two o'clock I had copied my last document in the Library stopped at a coffee shop near Madison. I took a booth to myself in the rear, and as soon as I'd ordered and sipped my coffee, I opened the briefcase again and took out my discoveries.

I was excited.

I had found a motive for malice.

Chapter 13

One thing I had unearthed in the Library was J. Forbes Munro's opening shot in the *Times* of late February, ten years ago:

"Sirs:

"Many things are crumbling from neglect and sabotage today, not the least of which are our freedoms, our confidence in the future, and even our esthetic standards. Men whom we thought could be counted on to guard the portals of the few surviving chapels of the spirit in which we could find some refuge from an encroaching barbarism have chosen to help the mob pry open the great doors. Our treasures are being looted, and what cannot be easily carried off has been smashed or vandalized.

"The betrayal is singularly apparent in the recent career of Patrick Player, lately lionized by our critical sentries for his spectacular 'comeback.' The last descendent of a distinguished stage family, Mr. Player effected a besotted and indifferent decline that saw him star as a barely tolerated has-been in the low-budget miasma of horror films and banal made-for-television morality

plays. If he has indeed 'come back,' it is as chief clown for the noveau fableaux. *Mr. Player, no longer content with trying to breathe life into pediculus screenplays, has elected to suffocate greatness under a pillow of snickers, guffaws, and sneers.*

"His latest depredation, Swift Sword, *is a much-admired remake of the original film, in which Mr. Player starred some years ago. His father, the late Malcolm Player, directed the original, which was co-produced by the then reputable Twin Dolphins company. The elder Player, through some forgotten studio deal, acquired controlling rights to the original, which he bequeathed to his son. His son has apparently made a studio deal himself, exchanging the rights to the original for a free hand to spray paint his father's masterpiece.*

"Coarse comedy has always existed, and perhaps always shall. Many who patronize it—as either actors or audience—are thick to the concept of the sublime, or conscious enemies of it. Their idea of a chapel of the spirit is a men's locker room or an institution for the insane. Communication to them of the sublime—or of the great or of the heroic or whatever other label we have to identify that cleanness of motive and ambition behind all of man's greatest, life-giving moments—is a wasted effort. They are also unresponsive to genuine comedy, though that subject deserves a separate essay. But what are we to say about an actor who once communicated the sublime, who seemed to understand it enough to give it that extra touch of endearing, unforgettable drama, when he chooses to join the ranks of his enemies? A cursory glance at his career can only lead one to the simple conclusion that his decision to appear in these films over the last few years is merely a sign of studied and premeditated capitulation.*

"Critics and observers have heralded Mr. Player's recent triumphs as marks of maturity, as proofs of wondrous diversity and scope. Filmgoers who rely on what modern critics say about this or that film or actor should not delude themselves. The things they read in contemporary reviews are the thrusts of rubber rapiers by men whose innermost chapels are actually dank cellars of malice. It is such cellars that make possible the* *praise Mr. Player has received. They recognize one of their own, they share his goal and end, which is to compel the rest of us to dine at a table laden with rotted food, while accepting Mr. Player and his admirers as worldly gourmands.*

"In closing, I contend that the sabotage Mr. Player has committed stems from nothing so innocent as ignorance, bad taste, or, as one blind critic called it, 'juvenile humor.' In every facet of the new Swift Sword *can be seen a conscious attempt to destroy and deface with indelible graffiti. This film is no accident; it was intended to be what it is. It is the product of genuine malice, adulterated only by the paradox that so much effort and money went into its creation. Malice offered publicly as art is a moral outrage that should not be rewarded, and ought to be boycotted, in this instance, at the box office.*

"Sincerely,

J. Forbes Munro

Professor of History, Ploughsmith College, New York."

I managed to read it twice, carefully, before the waitress brought my lunch. I was excited for so many reasons that I couldn't keep them on a leash. First, if I could write, this was what I would have said. I had felt it years ago when I gave up on Player and Rhodes and many others, and felt it last week in San Francisco when I saw *Falling Bodies*. I was excited, too, because Munro's remarks on malice reminded me of Kimberly Eames's.

If Munro was right, if malice drove Player to remake *Swift Sword*, it could also explain his crediting Munro with the screenplay of *Falling Bodies*. If, of course, the decision was his to make.

Munro's letter had run in the letters column of the *Times's* mammoth Sunday arts and entertainment section. It was a powerful letter indicting not only Player but also the paper's own film critics. There had been two favorable reviews of *Swift Sword* before Munro's letter appeared, along with one laudatory write-up on Player himself. A second write-up, on George Soquel, the picture's director, appeared in the same issue with the letter. I wondered why the letter appeared at all; possibly it was because of Munro's name and reputation; possibly the page editor was asleep at the wheel when it came time to select letters.

Whatever the reason, by the time the paper printed responses to Munro's letter, *Swift Sword*—the remake—had bombed. Ads for it had vanished. I'd checked through three weeks of the paper on the microfilm machine. I didn't think the picture's short run had anything to do with Munro's call for a boycott; it was simply a stinker that got bad word of mouth in spite of the imprimatur of the critics.

The most vitriolic responses to Munro's article had come from the critics themselves, though a syndicated columnist suggested that Munro suffered from "a form of intellectual gout."

The argument went back and forth for a while in the *Times*, and then Munro was apparently invited to submit an article to the *New Observer* on the subject of contemporary esthetics in film. In the article, Munro argued that a collapse of esthetics, a loss of the art of storytelling, and the aimless floundering of Hollywood were simply consequences of the collapse of literature, which in turn had been caused by the collapse of modern philosophy. For balance, the editors had invited an essay by a fellow who agreed on Munro's major points but stated that art was a social phenomenon, through which an individual could identify his place in society. I assumed the editors knew what he meant.

"More jitter juice?" asked the waitress.

As I nodded, I noticed that Golf Cap sat at the counter in front, his back to me, his head turned to watch people pass the diner's window.

I glanced at my watch; it was three-fifteen. I gathered my reading together, put it in the briefcase, left a tip, and went to the cashier to pay my check.

Then I walked over to the counter and told Golf Cap, "I hope Mr. Player is good for his money."

Golf Cap looked away, disgusted.

"I'll be seeing him tomorrow evening," I said. "I'll tell him you've done a great job."

Chapter 14

If all the tables holding the buffet were laid end to end, they'd have stretched for half a mile. That was just my imagination, of course, pressed and dulled by the movement and noise of over three hundred guests. There were a couple of squads of uniformed catering staff at the tables, which held the standard hors d'oeuvres, marinated partridge, champagne gaufrettes, sauternes sabayon, Viennese torte, and truffles, punctuated every ten or so feet of silver brocade by crystal bowls of fruit. Coffee and tea were dispensed from sparkling silver urns and served in delicate china. All the liquor—hard and soft—could have filled the water tank of a major midtown office building.

The lavishness of the buffet left me wondering what had been served the guests who were arriving from Elaine Card's mental illness banquet in Manhattan. Player must have suspected that dinner would be less than filling and not that appetizing. Many of the tuxedos and gowns whose wearers were piling food onto the black enamel plates at the buffet still wore tan tags pinned to them that read COFAMI (Committee for the Fight Against Mental Illness). Perhaps there had been more speechmaking than food. I knew from experience that thousand-dollar plates could be just as skimpy and indifferent as fifty-dollar plates.

The buffet room, which also served as a stand-and-chat cocktail room, was the first ballroom Player's guests were steered to after checking their wraps in the central hall, where they were given a buffet menu, an entertainment program, and a glossy brochure on Soundview. The brochure recounted the mansion's history and gently confessed that it was an officially designated state landmark that would not refuse tax-deductible donations for its upkeep.

Soundview was about one and a half times the size of City Hall in New York. It perched atop a hill that commanded vistas of all the Island and especially of the northern cliffs along the Sound and of the Connecticut shore far across the water. It was surrounded by twenty acres of wooded land. It had been built and occupied by a railroad man in the Nineteenth century, sold to a banker early in the Twentieth, and finally lost to Cedric Player, noted stage and film actor, in a pre-Depression poker game.

I hadn't expected Player to greet me at the door. He would know I was there, but it was nine-thirty now and the party might last until early morning.

He could just as easily have sent me a note with the answer to my question as send his invitation to this party. And he could have discussed his proposition, whatever it was, on the phone.

Around me were politicians, lobbyists, bankers, businessmen and their wives, business women, vice presidents of brokerage houses, screen and television stars, actors and actresses who were not stars but whose faces were familiar, retired newscasters, comedians, sports figures, representatives from the governor's and mayor's offices, artists, novelists, playwrights, several dozen anonymous couples, and a handful of photographers armed with flash cameras and video cameras.

Nobody recognized me, which made me happy. Nobody

except Ellen Romero, of the *Chronicle,* who had spotted me from clear across the buffet room but was too immersed in talk and eavesdropping to come ask me what I was doing here.

I'd had a light dinner in Manhattan, so I limited myself to a trifle with strawberry sauce and a glass of zinfandel before moving down the central hall to the second and larger ballroom. It was in the back of the mansion and overlooked the Sound. It was not quite as crowded as the first. An eight-man steel drum band was setting up on a stage as big as a high school auditorium's. A long, magnificently preserved mahogany bar was in the rear of the room, with four bartenders and a busy crew of waitresses. About fifty café tables formed a perimeter around what was intended to be the dance floor. Most of them were occupied, while some couples were already on the floor gyrating to the beat of taped French disco music that came from amplifiers on the stage.

I weaved my way through the tables and onlookers to the tall windows that looked out on the Sound. I could see a strip of lawn below, a fence around it, and flagstone steps lit by ground lights that snaked down to the side of the cliff to the beach and dock below. Out on the Sound were some slow-moving lights and beyond them the weak glow of Connecticut.

I went to the bar. It was a cash bar, proceeds going to the Soundview Preservation Foundation. I bought a vodka gimlet, and raised it in a silent toast to everything this party wasn't. I saw a vacant table near the wall, and sat down at it with the drink and a cigarette to ponder the imponderables. Player was nowhere in sight. But I saw Elliott Rhodes far across the room, talking with people I didn't recognize. His shoulders were still wide and powerful, and by the cut of his tuxedo jacket he seemed to have kept the taut, hair-trigger physique that had helped make him famous years ago.

Some attractive, unaccompanied women at other tables tried to catch my eye. I made it easy for them, and they quickly decided they didn't want to play. They couldn't classify me as a respectable roué, nor potential "nurturing father" material, nor as a domitable bachelor who could be whipped into shape and passed off as civic-minded. They lived in a lonely world where good men were hard to find. I couldn't agree with them more. Good men wouldn't be found here tonight.

A new number began over the amplifiers, Italian-sounding with a fast, cardiological beat to which a male singer added all the vowel sounds, in their proper order, no less. More guests were lured onto the dance floor.

I recognized some of them, especially Gerald F. St. Cyr, a New York representative in Congress who'd sponsored a bill that would force banks to provide free checking accounts and lower loan terms to the poor. He was in his late sixties and looked silly trying to be a twitchy twenty. His partner was a remarkable blonde in a slinky white gown who looked bored and embarrassed. Her pout was touching because it seemed so genuine. At a nearby table, someone said she was St. Cyr's daughter, Laurel. The congressman flashed his famous ivory grin as he danced around her like a rhythm-obsessed shadow-boxer. A flash went off, then another, and a photographer moved away to another part of the room.

Other guests of St. Cyr's age were on the floor trying to bring dignity to attempts to combine the fox trot and minuet. I didn't like anyone I saw. I glanced around the ballroom and tried to imagine what it must have been like a century ago, when a different breed of people enjoyed themselves here, and wondered if I'd have been happier then. I took a sip of the gimlet. I'd finish it, then find Player and get the hell out of here.

"Mr. Hanrahan?"

I looked up at the man who had spoken, and recognized Edwin Card, Manhattan real estate developer and tycoon. His face had appeared in the papers and on the covers of news magazines often enough. He was worth a few billion dollars. He was a fairly good-looking man, a few years older than I, and as trim as a tennis player. I didn't envy him his estimated worth; I merely mistrusted it. He was able to cut deals with the mayor and City Hall and Albany for forty-year tax rebates and assessment rollbacks and regulation suspensions when other developers and property owners could not. In other words, by grace of his connections and probable political graft, he had the freedom to plan and act, and others didn't.

"Yes?" I answered.

"My wife had the courtesy to call on you personally last week to attend this event. I want to advise you that the next time you speak to her, you do so with a civil tongue. And, I want to hear your apology for the rudeness, first to me, then to my wife."

I shrugged. "I spoke to her as civilly as I knew how, Mr. Card, to guarantee that there would be no next time."

"Excuse me?"

"She came to me. I didn't invite her."

Standing with Card was a little bald fellow, probably an attorney. Far across the room, near the entrance, stood Elaine Card, watching us.

I said, "She should have had the sense to guess that if I didn't respond to a paper invitation, her personal invitation might mean even less to me."

Card stared at me thoughtfully, then turned to glance briefly at his wife. He said, "Nevertheless, why did you feel it necessary to insult her?"

"Because it was apparent that subtlety would be wasted."

The little bald guy spoke up. "Mr. Hanrahan, Mr. Card is waiting for an apology."

I chuckled. "Then I hope he's wearing a comfortable pair of shoes."

Card held up a hand to silence the man. "To earn respect, Mr. Hanrahan, you must grant respect. Don't tempt me to lose what little I have for you. You'd regret it."

I sipped my gimlet. "There's the respect for a man of legitimate accomplishment. And there's the respect a crime boss expects from people under his thumb. The two stem from different motives: justice, and fear. Which do you expect from me?"

Card's stare lingered on me for a moment, then he turned away. "Come on, Phil, this is just wasting time."

I watched them retreat all the way back to the entrance. Card waved the little bald guy on, then stopped and appeared to start an argument with his wife. I'd have bet she'd told him a different version of my behavior that day.

"My congratulations, Mr. Hanrahan," a euphonious voice said behind me. "You gored the Minotaur in his own maze, and now he is punishing his ewe."

I turned. It was Elliott Rhodes. I fought an abrupt urge to turn away from the sight of him. The once-handsome face was sagging and puffy. His calm, studious blue eyes watched me from behind folds of tired flesh. I forced myself to say, "Good evening, Mr. Rhodes."

A sad smile twisted the actor's mouth. "You recognize me, but wish you hadn't, and won't be asking for an autograph. You're forgiven. I'm used to that." He paused to finish the few drams of brandy left in the glass goblet he held. "I was having a lackluster conversation with the Cards when she saw you. She was quite shocked to see you, and then eager to see you mashed under her husband's able heel. What *did* you say to her in your office?"

"Nothing I'd want to repeat."

"No matter," said Rhodes. "The diversion spared me from being invited to join one of Mrs. Card's many causes." He sat down at my table. "That was quite a little speech you gave, Mr. Hanrahan. I could see it took the pep from his pistol. A gem of extemporization, without a cue card in sight. I'm impressed."

"I have an organized mind."

"And a certain one, too. Can't say I've ever heard that sentiment before. Mr. Player asked me to hunt you down and tell you that he *will* see you sooner or later. Probably later. More people than he expected want to press his palm and massage his shoulders. I apologize in his stead."

I frowned. "How were *you* able to recognize me?"

"Why, Mrs. Card pointed you out with some surprisingly choice and heartfelt expletives. Nothing I'd want to repeat."

"How would you have recognized me otherwise?"

"Patrick gave me a very true description of you. And, he added, 'Look for the man whom no one else here reminds you of. He'll probably be alone.'" Rhodes paused. "I swear, that's what he said. Also a true description, once we deal out the Cards."

"Mr. Player is an observant fellow."

"As am I, Mr. Hanrahan."

Elliott Rhodes still had his voice, and his brittle wit and style. I wished I could still enjoy them. I might have smiled in appreciation, except that I knew that I was talking to a ghost. The steel drum bandleader had introduced his group while we spoke, but neither of us heard him. The band began its first number. I asked, gesturing with my empty glass to the ballroom, "Why a party after a banquet?"

The actor smiled. "Patrick was cornered by Mrs. Card some time ago and virtually pressed into becoming an honorary member of her board of directors. This is his way of letting off steam. He expected to need to, after the banquet. We all did. We endured six tedious speeches, an uninspired *table d'hôte*, and an embarrassingly egregious dramatization of a scene from *Of Mice and Men* by two not very well-trained actors, which Patrick introduced to a wary and weary audience. The skit was his own idea. I think he now regrets it. Everyone else did, though it received a fine, sincere applause—the kind you give a kindergarten class for performing *Swan Lake*—and perhaps a brief and obligatory airing on tomorrow evening's newscasts, to judge by all the cameras sitting in the wings." Rhodes studied his empty goblet. "So, why *not* a party? The least we've earned for taking our castor oil is a bowl of ice cream. That's what Patrick felt. It's his way of making amends."

"Castor oil," I mused. "That's good."

"Thank you."

The band was working its way up to a brisk, very complicated yet easy to listen to melody. I turned to watch them in action. They were very good.

Rhodes said, "It's clear that you're here under duress, Mr. Hanrahan. May I ask why?"

My throat was going dry, and I wanted another drink. But getting another might prompt Rhodes to invite himself to join me. I said, "I'm waiting for an answer to a question. And to hear a proposition from Mr. Player."

"I think I know something about his proposition—but, a question?"

I tilted my empty glass, asked casually, "Ever hear of J. Forbes Munro? The screenwriter who wasn't?"

Rhodes's eyes froze, and his great brow tightened. That might have been because we were suddenly surrounded by a half-dozen guests. Hands reached down and he shook them. As I looked around for a way out, I saw that the whole ballroom was packed and every table taken. People lined the walls, and the dance floor was filled to capacity. Rhodes's friends gave me a cursory glance, then ignored me. I stood up and squeezed through the group. From snatches of their excited talk, I learned that Rhodes last week had sold the rights to his Chimera Jones character to Twin Dolphins Productions for over two million dollars and a percentage of the box office.

Another hero was about to be fitted with a sea green wig and a bright red nose.

At the bar I ordered a gin and tonic and silently toasted the memory of the Elliott Rhodes I'd know long ago. I made my way to the entrance and stood for a while, watching guests mill in and out of the ballroom. There was nowhere for me to go, no one to see.

"Yond Cassius has a lean and hungry look; he thinks too much, such men are dangerous."

I recognized Player's voice and turned to see him come in with a group of guests. On his arm was a woman whose face I knew but couldn't connect with a name, while the others behind them were strangers.

"Mr. Hanrahan, I'm so glad you decided to come. I see Elliott over there. He gave you my message, didn't he?"

"Yes, he did."

"May I introduce my former wife, Moraga Hollister . . . And George Soquel, my favorite director at Twin Dolphins . . . Jonathan Sagassi, my associate at Autumn Harvest. I own that, you know, but Jon here runs it. . . . Selby Lane, my fellow hapless commuter in *Trackside*. Selby will be in my next film."

Player rattled off the names of the half-dozen other people accompanying him. I shook hands with some, merely nodded to others. Only Soquel, a florid-faced man with glasses, looked at me with interest.

"Ladies and gentlemen," continued Player, "this is Mr. Chess Hanrahan, eminent detective from Manhattan, a black sheep of New York Society, and a very patient man, indeed. He paid me a kindness recently and visited me backstage at *Trackside*—"

Soquel interrupted to say, "Oh! *This* is the one you were telling me about, Pat? Wasn't he—?"

Player cut him off with a smile. "Not now, George, not now. Leave me my surprises."

I asked, "Any news on that screenplay, Mr. Player?"

"Yes, and I'd like to talk to you about it and other matters this evening. As you can see, now wouldn't be opportune. Too many social chores."

Player had accosted me with a line from *Julius Caesar*. So, by way of reminder, I said, "You're right. I'm lean with purpose, hungry with curiosity. But, I can wait."

Player smiled charmingly. "Apt retort, sir, nicely paraphrased and doubtless fraught with a multitude of meanings."

Moraga Hollister tugged at his arm. "Come on, Patikins, there's St. Cyr and his cronies waving at us, and I want to say hello to his daughter. I've heard she gets vertigo when she's vertical, and it isn't very often, if certain men are to be believed." Moraga Hollister was a vaguely attractive woman half Player's age, an actress, I remembered now.

"Well," said Player with a sigh, shaking my hand again, "duty calls and we must be off! Please, enjoy yourself, Mr. Hanrahan, and we'll talk later."

Player and his entourage moved into the ballroom, and stopped. Player stared at something near the entrance. Although both ballrooms were done in a severe Deco style, there was a scattering of antique Eighteenth and Nineteenth century furnishings. One, a sturdy-looking, marble-topped side table, now held a collection of discarded glasses, cups and saucers and even a stack of black plates. Two men watching the band were leaning against it for support, pressing it to the paneled wall. Player said something to one of his party—Mr. Lelander of the Preservation Society—and then went on, while Lelander approached the guests who were abusing the table.

I finished my drink, put my glass on a tea wagon that sat outside the entrance, and strode down the central hall through the crowd in search of a restroom.

There was a red "No Smoking" sign in white letters glued to the wall next to the mirror, citing a Suffolk County ordinance and a warning of a fine. I lit a cigarette, exhaled a draught, and reached up to pry the sign from the immaculate green tile and dropped it in the waste bin below.

Chapter 15

"I'm waiting for you to change the wine into vinegar."

I was back in the first ballroom, which was less crowded now, buttering a scone at one of the buffet tables. Ellen Romero was across the room when I came in, standing by herself for once, busy writing in a little notebook. So I wasn't surprised to hear her voice beside me now. I gave her my first sincere smile of the evening.

I said, "I might, if I could."

Ellen nodded. "When you walked in here a minute ago, the look on your face reminded me of what Jesus must have looked like when he ascended the Temple steps to throw out the money-changers."

"I'm not sure I should be flattered by the comparison, Ellen. You know my views on that subject. More likely I'd have turned the Temple into a stock exchange and invited the money-changers back after the renovation."

"May I print that?"

"I wouldn't mind, but maybe your page editor might." I saw a vacant café table near the entrance, and jerked my head to it. "Get yourself a coffee and join me." I picked up my own and the scone and headed for it.

Ellen Romero caught up with me at the table. She was a tall, thin, elegant woman in her late fifties, with a Roman nose, scathing eyes, all-hearing ears—which dripped diamonds tonight—and a biting pen. She had been a top political reporter for the *Times* decades ago, then for the *Chronicle*. When she objected that news reporting was becoming news fabrication, she was nudged from one page to another until she accepted the gossip column. I'd asked her why she just didn't retire. "I can't be gotten rid of so easily," she said. "And I enjoy describing the people our bumfuzzled electorate vote for." And all she did was bring to her gossip column the same honesty, liveliness and curiosity with which she'd bedeviled several Washington administrations.

"All right, mister," she said now, "what are *you* doing here?" She sat down across from me, and turned her head once to glance at Elaine Card far in back, standing with her husband and other guests. "You didn't tell me last week you were coming."

"I didn't know it myself," I said. "I was invited by Player. I saw his play Saturday night and went backstage to pay my respects."

"I saw that play, too," said Romero. "It *is* a funeral, isn't it? Now, I picked up some talk here about you and Edwin Card trading blows over his wife."

"It didn't come to blows. I asked the man to keep her away from me." I finished my scone, then relented and gave her the whole story. She took out her tiny notebook and gold pen and scribbled away in shorthand. Her eyes shined greedily. Avarice became her. It was the only justice she was permitted.

"What's between you and our host?" she asked.

I shook my head. "I can't say anything about that now. I'm waiting to find out myself. Ask me what I think of the band." We could hear it in the other ballroom.

"Stubborn man. What do you think of the band?"

"It's a good band. I must give Player credit for having hired it."

Romero's eyes narrowed. "Credit for that—and for what else?"

"Nothing he'd be happy about. He's not sure he likes me."

Romero sighed, sipped her coffee, and asked, "Well, what else have you got for me?"

"Elliott Rhodes sold Chimera Jones to people who will put him in a funny wig and baggy pants. Beware of his squirting flower. It will contain the tear gas of conformity and social progress."

"Oh, that's not news! I read it last week in *Variety*! Though I think I can rewrite it the way you put it. You ape my style so well you're almost better at it than I am."

"Maybe you're aping *my* style," I teased her.

She made a face at me and busied herself in the notebook. Then she looked up. "You talked to Rhodes? I saw you with him."

"He did most of the talking." I filled Romero in on the highlights of my conversation with the actor, adding what I thought of him and what I used to think of him.

Romero paused in her note-taking to study me. "Now that you mention it, you *are* a little like he used to be. I hope you'll take that as a compliment."

I smiled. "I would, but I'm not sure it would flatter him."

The crowd in the central hall was thinning out. Two Preservation Society staffers came out lugging the antique table that had been in jeopardy. They set it down in front of an oak door marked "Screening Room: Private." One man opened the door, and they carted the desk in. I got a glimpse of a large room with tall bookshelves, Tiffany lamps, deep leather club chairs. There were pictures on the walls, not portraits. The men came out and closed the door. There was no sign of a lock.

Romero said, "I talked with Tony Heskett. He's about to begin shooting his next meat cleaver, *Bury the Butcher*."

"The *Chronicle*'s front page is horror story enough for me," I said.

"Our host even broke silence and told me something about *his* next picture. Have you read that big bestseller yet, *The Thankful Corpse*?"

Romero was referring to a novel by *noir* writer Richard Welling, in which a private eye is hired by a murder victim to exonerate his murderer and pin the blame on a complete stranger. The private eye collects a big fee for destroying evidence, not collecting it. The *Chronicle*'s book reviewer had called *The Thankful Corpse* a "*tour de force* metaphysical statement of penultimate proportions, because the next best comment on the contemporary human condition is to say nothing."

I gave Romero what I knew was a strange look. "Somehow I missed it. What about it?"

"Our host is going into pre-production this winter."

"Who's doing the screenplay?" I asked, suddenly interested.

"Welling himself. George Soquel to direct, Leonard Sproule and Albert Grunnian to produce. Starring Player, Elliott Rhodes, and Selby Lane. Another Twin Dolphins gem coming your way. To be shot entirely in New York out of the Astoria studios."

I mused, more to myself than to Romero, "They haven't appeared together since *Swift Sword*."

"Who?"

"Player and Rhodes."

"What about it?" asked the columnist, now alert.

"Just a thought that slipped out."

"How would *you* know what they've appeared in together?"

I didn't answer.

"Hmmm." Romero tapped her gold pencil on her open notebook. "Well, they're thick as thieves now."

Ellen Romero left me a while later to join Phoebe Meadows, society columnist for the *Times*, and together they stalked the

Cards and their coterie to the second ballroom. I finished my coffee and lingered in the central hall near the oak door. When I thought no one was looking, I opened the door and slipped into the room.

I closed the door gently behind me. It fit so snugly in the strips that when the latch snapped home all evidence of the party—the hundreds of voices, the clink of glasses, the clatter of heels on the marble floors, even the steel drums—ceased to exist. My ears were bathed in absolute silence. I stood in the darkness for a moment, savoring it. Then I felt along the wall behind me and found the light switch.

The first thing I saw was the picture I'd glimpsed from the ballroom. It was a framed, enlarged still of the Player family patriarch, Cedric Player, in a pirate costume: arms folded, a flintlock pistol in one hand, a cutlass in the other. He wore a wicked grin. The still, according to a plaque beneath the frame, was from one of his earliest silent pictures, *Morgan of the Main.*

The walls were covered with stills from Cedric Player's other pictures. Further back in the room were bookshelves, tables laden with memorabilia, and a screening area of old, velvet-lined theater seats and a fixed screen. On my left, a mammoth cherry desk and floor-to-ceiling bookshelves created a small study.

The room was full of art, but the photo-history of the Player family interested me most. After Cedric had come Malcolm, who could not act but demonstrated skill with cameras. His father hired him out to many of the independent film companies active in New York and New Jersey. When the industry shifted to California, the Players followed. By the time he was twenty, Malcolm Player was an accomplished and innovative cameraman. When he began directing, his first sound picture was a production of Robert Browning's "My Last Duchess," starring his father as the Duke and his father's current mistress, Dedra Landis, as the late Duchess. Later had come *Drums*, featuring Malcolm's son Patrick. The boy had been groomed for an acting career. The last photograph of

Malcolm Player showed him standing with his arms around his father and son on location in Spain for *Drums*. He looked his happiest in that photograph.

I followed Patrick Player's life for a while. A few of the photos evoked pleasanter thoughts of Player than I'd had recently. Several showed him in the roles of Hamlet and Richard the Third at the Royal Academy of Dramatic Arts in London.

And one photo abruptly brought me back to the present. It partly answered the question of why Player had invited me here.

It showed Player as a student at Vickers Preparatory Academy, near Boston, in a production of Oscar Wilde's *The Importance of Being Earnest*. He was in Edwardian costume, faced off to exchange barbs with another character. The plaque beside the photo read: "During his four years at Vickers, Patrick Player appeared in many of the group's productions with future biographer J. Forbes Munro, then an ardent thespian, co-director of many of the Society's stagings, and author of skits and one-act dramas and comedies that drew the attention of many Boston critics. Here Player and Munro trade *bon mots* in the last act of Wilde's satire on manners. Malcolm Player, when not busy directing a new film, often attended his son's appearances."

There was a second Vickers photograph, a class graduation picture. Six heads were neatly circled in a group of forty seniors. The plaque read: "Many of Player's classmates would go on to distinguish themselves in a variety of careers: . . . J. Forbes Munro, biographer and essayist. . . ." I stopped reading. The other names meant nothing to me.

Yet, backstage at the Gilpin Theater, Patrick Player had had to think to recall Munro's name. They had to have been good friends once. And a good friend could turn into a worst enemy if a serious betrayal occurred between them.

Chapter 16

I spent the rest of the evening twiddling my mental thumbs. I peeked into the crammed and noisy second ballroom a number of times, only to see Player at a different table each time talking to a new collection of friends and admirers. Gerald St. Cyr, the congressman, was very busy on the dance floor, but the band was too good for him and he couldn't keep up. His pouty daughter had attached herself to a handsome man at a far table. Elliott Rhodes circulated among the guests, many of whom seemed not to know him even though he seemed to know them. Camera flashes winked continuously like a subdued fireworks display, while television people with video cameras roamed both ballrooms.

In the central hall, I happened upon a group that was being entertained by the two actors who'd done the scene from *Of Mice and Men* at the banquet. They were doing it again, but this time as an improvisational comedy skit. The group thought it was screamingly funny. Ellen Romero, who stood nearby, was busy taking notes. Her column was going to be rich in anecdotes for the next few editions of the *Chronicle*.

In the first ballroom I encountered old friends of my father, Mr. and Mrs. Lurie. I allowed myself to be roped into conversation with them, just to fight off my impatience with Player. Hal Lurie had retired years ago as chief executive of the country's largest warehousing machinery maker, and my father had set up a very comfortable stock portfolio for him. It enabled the Luries to live high over Park Avenue and to play Society by throwing money at every humanitarian appeal that came in the mail. I hadn't seen them in years and so we briefed each other on our lives. I mentioned that I'd gone to Europe last spring.

"You got to Paris, didn't you, Chess?" asked Mrs. Lurie. "How did you like it? Hal and I flew there for a week just last month. Our sixth time! It's so charming and we never get tired of it."

"I got tired of it," I said. "There's too much *noirceur* in the City of Light for me."

The Luries looked sad for me and delicately changed the subject. They had heard the Berlin Philharmonic at Carnegie Hall recently and so we talked about music for a while, and then Mrs. Lurie put a gentle hand on my wrist. "Darling, what *are* you doing here tonight? We didn't see you at the banquet."

"That's because I wasn't there," I answered. "I'm here to see Patrick Player on business."

"How exciting! Are you going to do some sleuthing for him?"

"Perhaps he's already done it," said a voice I recognized. Elliott Rhodes had joined us. I made the introductions. Mrs. Lurie was thrilled.

Rhodes said to me, "Patrick asked me to fetch you. He's waiting for us in the screening room."

"Well, stay in touch, Chess," said Mrs. Lurie, moving away with her husband. "Give us a call some time." She looked bewildered, and Hal looked intrigued.

Rhodes paused long enough to nod hello to someone in back of me, then asked, "*Are* you going to do some sleuthing for Patrick?"

"Maybe I've already done it."

Rhodes hummed in doubt. "You asked me hours ago about an imaginary screenwriter. We were rudely interrupted by a gaggle of well-wishers before I could answer."

"I asked if you'd ever heard of J. Forbes Munro."

Seeing a path through the crowd, I took it. Rhodes followed my lead. "Can't say I have, Mr. Hanrahan. What picture did he do?"

"That's just my point. He didn't." Rhodes looked confused. I said, "You sold Chimera Jones to Twin Dolphins. Don't you care what they'll do to him?"

Rhodes shrugged. "There wasn't much demand for him in his original form. His mien and panache are ill-suited to today's style of hero. Why do you ask?"

"You know they'll turn him into a joke, and his enemies as well. Revere nothing, fear nothing."

Rhodes smiled. "He was something of a joke from the beginning. The critics never liked him. He was kiddy fare for adults of arrested maturity—so they all said. Fun to do, too. It's time he went through the initiation ritual and became a plausible person. A whole new generation needs to be fed its brand of iconic pap. Whole grain mush," said Rhodes, a distant regret in his voice. "Just add water and stir."

He was watching me with more than idle curiosity. The blue eyes were alert and cautious. I stopped to face him. "Funny you should mention an initiation ritual. That was one of my favorite episodes. Remember? When Jones is pitted against a group of nihilist spies and traitors? The group insisted that he join them, and he insisted he didn't. I think I was twelve when that aired. You've no idea how much it helped me face the next few years of my life. It made so many things clear in my mind. Of course, I didn't realize the importance of that episode then as much as I do now. Thanks."

Rhodes's eyes relaxed in the repose of knowledge. "So," he said softly, "that's what you're all about." He smiled. "You're welcome, Mr. Hanrahan. But—believe me, Chimera Jones was a joke from the moment I conceived of him. Accept that, and your present disappointment won't be so painful. And you won't take such personal exception to what will happen to him in the future."

I shook my head. "No, you're lying. And if you weren't, it wouldn't change anything. I saw what I saw. If it was pap, I'd have known it and not bothered with Jones." I grinned. "Children are hard to fool, Mr. Rhodes. They're very sensitive to frauds. You weren't a fraud then. What happened? Did it get too lonely?"

Rhodes smiled his deadliest smile, a menacing smile, the smile I'd liked so much when he was Chimera Jones. "It became quite arctic, Mr. Hanrahan." The great brow frowned. "Let's not keep Patrick waiting." He turned curtly and walked away in the direction of the screening room.

Patrick Player sat at his father's desk at the far end of the exhibition room, leaned back in the wing chair, one arm outstretched with a hand on a brandy snifter that sat on an ochre coaster on the desk. A column of cigarette smoke weaved placidly from the ceramic ashtray. Two large envelopes sat on the desk. His eyes had been closed when we came in, and remained closed as we made our way through the room. He looked as though he were enjoying a momentary solitude—just as I had earlier—or preparing for a role worthy of his profile. He opened his eyes only when my jacket arm brushed against the side of a bookcase. He had been either completely oblivious to our approach, or pretending.

"Ah! Mr. Hanrahan! We talk at last! Elliott, please stay. This may interest you as much as it will me. Brandy?" Player picked up a bottle of Napoleon. I shook my head. Rhodes smiled and nodded. As he poured another snifter, Player asked, with a mischievous glance at me, "Have you been enjoying yourself this evening?"

I sat down on the black leather couch. "Academically, yes. Actually, no. This is not my kind of crowd."

Player handed the snifter to Rhodes, and resumed his seat. "I wonder if you have any kind of crowd." He sipped his brandy and studied my face. "Why do I think you expected to witness scenes of wild hedonism here tonight, such as Tilley Lace bathing in a tub of milk and honey under the main chandelier, and giddy guests dunking for apples in great bowls of Lafite Rothschild? But perhaps you see more vital kinds of debauchery and silliness. I'm glad you weren't disappointed."

"Beware, Patrick," said Rhodes in mock warning. He stood aside between the desk and the couch. "That's meat for the tiger, but your arm will do just as well."

"What do you mean?" asked Player, amused.

"Our friend here holds some unique grudges. You'll see."

Player turned back to me. "What flibbertigibbet itches you, Mr. Hanrahan?"

"Can we get on with our business? I'm tired and in no mood to play rubber rapiers with you."

Both Player and Rhodes frowned. Player mused, "Rubber rapiers? Where have I heard that phrase before?" He drummed fingers on the desk. He put out his cigarette, finished his brandy, and then slapped his hands flat on the morocco leather blotter. "No matter. First, my proposition, Mr. Hanrahan. My next picture will be a production of Richard Welling's *The Thankful Corpse*, the detective novel. No doubt you've heard of it, if not read it. It's been promoted and advertised so much that even someone with the worst case of dyslexia would recognize the title instantly. Anyway, I'm to play the murdered mobster, Mr. Pluennkey, while Elliott here will portray the eccentric gumshoe, Tom Turlock. And you've already met Selby Lane, who's to play the hapless accountant and imaginary murderer. It's an unusual story, a tat too metaphysical for the movie-going public, but the author has agreed to an excision of the more exotic story elements. Mustn't tax their minds, the poor dears.

"Now, I've spoken with Mr. Welling—who couldn't be here tonight, he's attending some kind of writers' conference in Iowa—and with Mr. Soquel and to a number of my other colleagues, and they're all agreeable to hiring you on as a technical consultant for this project. They all thought it was an inspired idea. You are, after all, a fairly well-known private investigator. You may be able to bring your experience to bear on Mr. Welling's script and suggest ways to tighten it up or add some spice to it. He's been very flexible in that matter from the beginning."

Player paused for a moment, waiting for a reaction. "We might even be able to find a small part in the picture for you, say, a brief cameo as yourself, or a short speaking part in one of the key scenes in one of the minor roles. You won't even need to fly to Hollywood or interrupt your own work schedule. The picture will be shot entirely in Manhattan out of Astoria." Player beamed. "How does that strike you, Mr. Hanrahan?"

It was quite a proposition. In fact, it was so outrageous that I sat for a moment, expecting Player to sweeten the pot even more. Rhodes was as surprised as I was. Apparently Player hadn't confided in him about it. He stood looking at the Persian rug beneath his feet, trying to digest Player's words. But then his expression changed, and he grinned faintly.

Player gave me time to reply. He slid forward one of the envelopes, opened it, and took out what looked like a contract. He flipped through its pages idly, then closed it and put it aside. "I took the liberty of having a contract prepared, Mr. Hanrahan. I've already signed it. All it needs is your ink, and by Friday you should receive an advance large enough to cover your office expenses for the next five years."

Of course, he was serious about the proposition. He'd made a genuine offer. I believed he was making it in good faith and would honor the terms of the contract if I signed it.

So I sat there and studied him and waited for him to triumphantly fan his card hand on the table.

Player studied me in turn, and saw what Rhodes had seen earlier. There was the beginning of a smile in his eyes, but still he looked solemn. "'Tis time to fear when tyrants seem to kiss.' That's the expression on your face now, Mr. Hanrahan. I did *Pericles* once, a long time ago, in London at the Academy. I didn't do him very well, and my instructor concurred. But if I'd matched that line with your look now, I might have salvaged something of value from the exercise. It might have even changed the course of my career."

"Who wrote the screenplay for *Falling Bodies*?" I asked.

The solemnity in Player's face faded and his features hardened. He took the contract and ripped it in two. Then he reached for the second envelope and extracted its contents. He studied the mass of paper for a moment before he said, "Elliott, would you please pass this to Mr. Hanrahan?"

Rhodes silently obliged him, and he handed me the paper. It was a manuscript of onion skin pages, old enough to have an inch-wide border of yellow on the stop sheet, which read, in neatly typed letters: "*The Stars Within: A Story of Galileo. A Screenplay by J. Forbes Munro. Dedicated to Patrick Player.*"

Chapter 17

*P*layer said, *"I wrote the screenplay. Munro wrote* that.*"*

I leafed with curiosity through the slick pages. "But the screenplay was based on this script," I remarked.

"Without question," answered Player. "Most of the best lines in *Falling Bodies* came from that script. Not the comedic ones. Munro had not intended any of his dialogue to be humorous. Edifying, perhaps, or dramatic, daring, heart-breaking, challenging, or in some rare instances, even mildly amusing. But never funny." He seemed to smile in fond memory. "Munro's directorial instructions—camera angles and tracking, stage business and such—are markedly amateur, but those can be forgiven. But it is a remarkable script, nonetheless. Almost a verse drama. No one writes those anymore."

"Yet last Saturday night you couldn't quite recall his name."

Player shrugged. "I'd just come offstage, Mr. Hanrahan. My mind was in a jumble. And it's been five years since I last laid eyes on the screenplay in your hands." His blasé smile said I could believe that or not.

I didn't. "This is a drama, not a farce. Am I correct?"

"Do you mean this moment of ours, or Munro's opus there?" Player laughed once. "Of course, you mean the *opus*. You are correct in that assumption."

"And Munro wrote this in his and your last year at Vickers Prep."

Player nodded. "That very spring. He'd intended it to be a farewell gift to me on graduation day. But I talked him into selling it to me, instead, or rather to my father's own firm, Parthenon Films." Player nodded to the typescript in my hand. "Stapled to the back of that is a copy of the receipt. 'Sold to Parthenon Films, one screenplay by J. Forbes Munro.' There's the title and subject and page length and all the other particulars. For five hundred dollars. My father, of course, thought it was an encouraging transaction for Munro and me. Even though I was only seventeen at the time, I was technically an agent for my father's firm, and the man was always reminding me to be on the lookout for new properties. He approved of the purchase. His signature is there along with Munro's and my own." Player paused. "Of course, I promised Forbes that one day I would produce his story, perhaps even star in it. And, of course, a few years later I'd forgotten all about it. So, apparently, had Forbes. In the course of researching the material for his screenplay, he became addicted to history—for which he previously had only a passing interest—and dramaturgy fell by the wayside."

"He dedicated it to you."

"Touching gesture. Also an uninvited one."

"And you turned it into a farce."

Player sat with his hands folded on the blotter. He answered my questions and statements as though he'd thoroughly briefed himself for every conceivable objection. "My father owned the property. When he died, I inherited all rights to it. And all privileges."

"Did you keep track of each other after Vickers?"

"For a while. Then we lost touch. Perhaps even the memory. It happens quite often with best friends, I've observed."

"What did you think of his screenplay? What do you think of it now?"

"Aside from its obviously amateurish conception and structure, it was a magnificent idea that might have, with work, become a definitive screenplay."

"But you chose not to do that."

"No."

"Why not?"

"Can't you guess, Mr. Hanrahan? You've guessed everything else."

"You wanted to pay him back for starting a controversy about your remake of *Swift Sword*."

Player shook his head in appreciation. "You were right, Elliott. He has done some sleuthing." Rhodes had moved back into the shadows, as though he expected to see a fist fight. "Remarkable, isn't it? After all these years. All those critics. All the opportunities for someone to make the connection. Not a single person saw the bare truth—until now."

Player turned to me again. "Confession time, again. I knew exactly what you were driving at in my dressing room last Saturday, Mr. Hanrahan. The only reason you could have to ask that question was if you were certain that Forbes couldn't have written the screenplay to *Falling Bodies*. So you decided to untangle the circumstances—shall we call it an esthetic paradox?—and get confirmation from me." The actor paused to pour himself another brandy. He offered the bottle to Rhodes, who shook his head. "Yes, I wanted to pay Forbes back for that controversy. He had no right to judge me. He put me on a pedestal I had always been reluctant to climb. Nearly drove me mad at Vickers. He was worse than my father. He worshipped me—damn him. And when you're young, and that happens to you, well, you're naïve enough to reciprocate. You oblige, and ask him to raise the hoop higher. And when Forbes left my life, and we forgot each other, the hoop fell. I fell with it. No one was able to hold it as high as he did. I think he suspected, even back then, that I would never be strong enough to hold it up myself. He should have known better. If he was so damned brilliant, why couldn't he have seen that? Why couldn't he understand? Instead, he sits down and scribbles something out and dedicates it to me."

Rhodes spoke up in his corner of darkness, addressing Player. "Besides, the remake was just an affectionate spoof. No harm in that. Can't be serious about everything all the time. It would make you a nervous wreck, drive you to drink and so on. I speak from experience."

I shook my head. "Where's the affection in ridicule?"

Player's features hardened again. "No, Elliott, let's be honest about this. Mr. Hanrahan is right. There is no affection in ridicule." He faced me. "You can't have learned *this* in your sleuthing. Do you know who was responsible for the original *Swift Sword*? Forbes! In his junior year at Vickers he read a historical novel by Herbert Galante, *This Green Isle*. He gave it to me to read, saying it would make a great film. There was a character in it he thought I could play very well. I read the novel, agreed with him, and passed it on to my father. Four years later he made that picture. *Swift Sword*. I got a letter from Forbes after its release, thanking me for a job well done. That was the last I ever heard from him—until his *Times* letter, addressed to the world. Quite embarrassing."

I'd been asking my questions as though Player was a slot machine that kept giving nothing but sevens. "Why did you do the remake?"

"Because I was trying to climb back out of a hole. I sold the rights to it to the studio, and that's what they did with it. I didn't care anymore what was done with it. I'd even forgotten who was responsible for the original, until some studio clerk reminded me. No, that's not true, either. I hadn't forgotten, but Forbes and that time and what everything else meant to me seemed so far away. Lost in time and half-remembered friendships."

"Until you read Munro's letter in the *Times*."

"Until that letter, which Mr. Soquel brought to my attention. After an instant surge of anger, I thought nothing of it. We were no longer friends, and Forbes seemed to have evolved into a boring, quibbling pedant. But it did prompt some guilty souls in Hollywood to talk about forming ethics committees and independent boards to guarantee or reward story integrity. Nothing ever came of the chatter and nothing ever could. But every time the subject came up, the remake and I were either the focal points or the catapult. It was humiliating, and disgusting given some of the people who tried to rub it in. I resolved to do something about it, to throw it all back in their faces—and Forbes's face. I could do nothing immediately. I had other commitments. I had to wait a few years."

"So I noticed," I said. I lit a cigarette. "In *Falling Bodies*, all of Kimberly Eames's scenes were shot separately, weren't they?"

Player smiled in appreciation. "A studious observation, Mr. Hanrahan. My compliments. Yes, that's true. I had to be careful with her. I insisted that Mr. Soquel keep her apart from the others as much as possible, at rehearsals, during meetings, on the set, at get-togethers. That was easy to accomplish, since we both knew a little about Miss Eames and she wasn't the most sociable person anyway. She was so starry-eyed and worshipful and so damnably private. You found her difficult to work with, too, didn't you, Elliott?"

"Difficult, but worth the agony. Everyone involved in *Fraction of Fear* thought so. She could have gotten away with the usual prima donna antics, but she didn't even try. She worked, and then was gone until the next shoot."

"If she'd learned what we were really up to," said Player, "I'm certain that she would have risked fines and other penalties for breach of contract, rather than finish her scenes for *Falling Bodies*. What I managed to do for her in that picture was my way of paying back her worshipping movie-going public. It was a separate vendetta. Please, Mr. Hanrahan, understand that, and I had no premonition that she and Forbes would ever meet. Though I ought to have suspected that such a union of wounded spirits might occur."

I stood up and paced for a moment, cigarette in one hand, the Munro typescript in the other. "So, your purpose was to kill two birds with one stone. Munro and Eames."

"If you wish to put it so crudely," Player answered. "With Forbes, I couldn't in good conscience deny him credit when I'd used so much from his material. Many other people in my position wouldn't have bothered with such an acknowledgement. It's one of the banes of writing for Hollywood. Whatever one writes under studio contract as an outside hack is no longer one's property. So I gave him full credit, and did some fancy talking to convince the studio to honor him, and not me, and to ensure that he was paid for it with a very generous cut of the box office. And with Miss Eames, well, I do so dislike goddesses who wrinkle their noses at the human in us all." Player paused when I turned to face him. "I tried to *make* her, you know. Tried my whole repertoire of guile and charm. But there was no laying hands on her, except in front of cameras. A phenomenon like her must be terribly frigid and lonely."

I took a drag on my cigarette. "Why have you told me all this?"

Player shrugged lightly. "You seem to be a man of justice, Mr. Hanrahan. I could see that last Saturday night. Give me some credit. Perhaps you see justice going begging here. Now that you know the truth, I'd be interested to see what you could possibly do about it. Of course, there's nothing you could do that would hurt me. Nothing legal, that is. Perhaps you will insult me, or call me names I've already called myself." He paused. "I think as much of you as I have thought of Forbes and Miss Eames. I didn't want you to go away empty handed."

"Considerate of you," I said.

"Thank you. You're closer to Forbes than you are to her, in my mind, though a cruder version of him. You see, that one single letter of his in the *Times* was enough. That letter, with its libelous insinuations, its stinking judgmental tone, its digs at a life of disappointment and torment—*my* life, mind you, not his. I didn't live up to *his* expectations! What did he expect me to do? Check into a monastery and wait until Hollywood was struck dumb by some vengeful Renaissance?"

"You could have fought it," I said. "You had the weight and the punch. You could have started that Renaissance yourself."

Player scoffed. "No, not as candidate for Memory Lane. The weight and punch were spent. Besides, I grew tired of being the measure of other people's candles. I had a career to reclaim and revive."

I put my cigarette out in the ash stand next to the couch. "She was right. It *was* malice. That's all it was."

"Don't look so disappointed," Player said, rising. He turned away to face some of his father's photographs. "It's a common enough human emotion. I admit to harboring it. Even to nurturing it. Its sole value rests on how effectively one can exploit it. I can assure you, it's more satisfying than murder."

I glanced at Rhodes, who stood watching us with a mask of neutral curiosity. He looked in another direction. I leafed through Munro's script, hungry to read it. I said, "May I have a copy of this?" Player turned to face me again. "For my own edification, of course. I'll read it, and see just how much you sabotaged Munro's story, and you can satisfy yourself by imagining how much grief you've caused me. It'd be another payback you could chalk up and cackle over."

Player reached across the desk and snatched the script from my hands. "Certainly not! Find your own copy, if you can!" He smacked the manuscript down on the blotter. "Even if Forbes kept a copy of it all these years, she won't let you see it. And don't bother trying to wheedle one from Twin Dolphins. Studios are very stingy with their properties, especially one of this nature."

"They should be," I said. "Tell me why you invited me here, Player. It couldn't have been just to pull your cruddy little motive out of your hat."

"I wasn't quite sure of the reason for your interest, Mr.

Hanrahan. And I had to have you here. You had suspicions, and so had I. You sought confirmation, and so did I. Now we both know."

"Called off your spy yet?"

Player chuckled and sat down. "Oh, so you spotted him? I pulled Mr. Totten off this morning. How long had you known about him?"

"Long enough," I said. "Who tipped you off to me? Carol Holvick?"

"Inadvertently. She'd checked some reference books in her office after you spoke with her, and was surprised to see Forbes's name in a directory of screenwriters. She called Twin Dolphins, and her call was forwarded to me. I charmed her into telling me your interest in Forbes. Then I called Miss Eames's agent and told him to warn her that the sly Chess Hanrahan was on the prowl. I didn't do that for her benefit, but to make it harder for you. I appreciate her convent-like silence, you know. It's one of my unexpected accomplishments. Finally, I called Mr. Totten, discreet investigator, and put him to work—he's been on a studio retainer for years—and had someone in Twin Dolphins's research office in New York do a quick record check on you. By Saturday afternoon, I knew all I needed to know about the man I sooner or later expected to meet."

I sighed. "Well, I guess that's it. I got what I came for. Good night." I turned and began to walk away. I wanted to hit the bastard, of course, to break a few bones. For everything he'd ever done, and thought, and said, concerning Munro and Kimberly Eames. I think he knew how I felt. Perhaps he would welcome a beating, accept it as atonement. But this was his house, and I could be charged with battery, and Player would carry on in his work like a midnight saboteur.

"What?" exclaimed Player behind me, genuine surprise in his voice. "No memorable parting shots at me?"

"No," I said, and left.

Chapter 18

I *stood* *by* *the* *entrance* *to* *the* *second*
ballroom to listen to the steel drum band. For the first time this
evening the crowd was an abstraction I didn't feel an urge to
examine. I had what I came for. I turned reluctantly from the
music and strode down the central hall to retrieve my coat.

At the cloakroom near the main entrance I handed the
attendant my plastic disk and waited for him to find my coat.
Elliott Rhodes emerged from the crowd and sauntered up to
me, a new drink in his hand.

"I enjoyed the duel of wills, Mr. Hanrahan," he said with
tentative friendliness. "Patrick, too, I imagine, in spite of the
acrimony. He relishes that kind of repartee. It's a vanishing art,
you know. The new generation of thespians has advanced little
beyond the style of Dick and Jane."

The attendant came with my coat and handed it over the
counter. I gave her a tip. As I slipped into the coat, Rhodes said,
"What will you do now? You're a detective. You've acquired
knowledge. How could you possibly put it to any earthly use?"

It was none of his business, and I didn't like his interest. I replied, "Oh, I don't know, Mr. Rhodes. Maybe I'll write a book. *The Rise and Fall of the House of Player*. Something like that. There's always a market for Hollywood scandal stories." I paused. "Then Player could make a Gothic movie of it. I'm sure he could do a great parody of his grandfather. Or even of his great-grandfather."

Rhodes gave me an odd look, and glanced away briefly. Then he said, "You know, Patrick pulled his punches with you. He was terribly broken when his son Brett died in a car accident. He was as talented as his father. Patrick hasn't entirely recovered from it. Then his wife divorced him and took half his assets. That hurt him, too. Pain and sorrow can move a man to do strange things. Turn him around completely. He could have tried to play on your sympathy. He didn't."

I shook my head. "No. I think he knew I had no sympathy for him to play on. So he didn't bother. Besides, I think it's obvious that he's acquired a taste for inflicting pain over expressing it."

Rhodes hummed in thought. "Well . . . perhaps you're right. I just hope you don't do something rash. Such as write a book."

"What's it to you?"

"I've had to hitch my wagon to his star, Mr. Hanrahan. It's not my preferred mode of travel through filmdom, but he and I vaguely resemble two peas in a pod—as you've no doubt deduced for yourself."

This time I glanced away. "You had your own star, once."

I headed for the door, and Rhodes followed along.

"It went out, my star," he said. "Then people left me in the dark with a suddenly antediluvian image and passed me by. The business is very cruel, Mr. Hanrahan. Very brutal. You have no idea."

I stopped to button up my coat. "Yes, I do. I got a big sample of it tonight. Well, there's nothing I can do to Player. There's no law that covers his kind of crime."

Rhodes said something else to me, but I paid him no

attention. I could no longer stand the sight of him. I pulled on my gloves and went through the doors out into the cold.

When the air hit my face, a weight seemed to lift from my mind and I didn't feel as tired. I glanced at my watch: it was two-thirty. There was a light wind off the Sound and it had blown in a fog. Some people followed me out; two couples squeezed into a green and blue cab that had pulled up under the portico. Groups of chauffeurs huddled and talked as they stood near a line of limousines that stretched from the portico back into the fog. More people came out of the place, and I moved on, heading for the parking lot. I found my car, pulled out, and drove off for a cautious descent down the long driveway through the soup to Luther Lane.

Rhodes was wrong, or bluffing in the belief I wasn't as well acquainted with Player's career as he was. Player's decline had begun long before his son died, more than a decade before. But that gave me only a slightly stronger reason to dislike Player. It didn't matter. . . .

I had the answers I had come for, and I felt cheated. I had expected a stupendous revelation concerning the Munro screen credit. Something devious, insidious and complex. This was small, and cheap and seedy.

Kimberly Eames had been right. At the root of the injustice was malice: the vengeful, bitter anger of a dwarf. Her husband's rebuke had exposed Player not only to others but to himself. Player was too intelligent, too aware, too observant to be ignorant of what he'd done. And would continue to do. If he'd had any doubts, Munro had resolved them for him. There was the malice expressed by the ignorant, and the malice expressed by the knowledgeable. You could forgive the first, but not the second.

I was tired, but at home I removed my dinner jacket and slipped into my robe and sat on the couch with a brandy. I propped the Magellan ad of Kimberly Eames against the wall near a window and studied it for a long while. She was the key to any justice I could devise. Exhaustion caught up with me. I stretched out on the couch and closed my eyes. At some point I felt Walker's paws land on my chest and his purring body curl up on it. The purring helped to send me over.

In the morning, as I shaved, I had another go at the thing. I didn't think Patrick Player's corruption had anything to do with his being a third generation actor and rich to boot. I was a fourth generation Hanrahan, and rich to boot. We'd both had choices to make. If mine had been like Player's, I could have commiserated with him and Rhodes, fallen in with them for spiritual warmth. We'd have had a merry old time being tired and savvy and cynical as hell. And since all three of us would be well-read and bright and quick with our tongues, we could have salted our cynicism with aphoristic crystals of wit, and bemoaned the demise of repartee along with everything else.

I wondered for a moment which judgment of Munro's had hurt Player the most: the moral or the esthetic? All my esthetic judgments were based on some moral criterion. A moral judgment couldn't be escaped. I believed Player realized that as much as I did. When I was a homicide detective, I'd encountered criminals who were so hardened that they were dead to any moral judgment. Morality was an artifice to them, or an imposition.

But a man like Player could only feign indifference to a moral judgment, and not very well, regardless of his acting skills.

I looked down at the plaza next door. It was a busy Thursday morning on Second Avenue. No one was sitting in the plaza, and there was no blue Volvo parked on either side of the Avenue. Farewell, Mr. Totten, alias Golf Cap. I realized that something was missing from everything I had learned so far. I stood for a moment, trying to conjure it up, but it wouldn't come. I scratched Walker's head by way of goodbye, and left for the garage and Forest Hills Gardens.

Chapter 19

It seemed like years had passed since I last walked beneath the pedestrian bridge that formed a boundary of the Forest Hills Gardens square. The place still retained that arrested-in-time quality. The Gardens had been new when Cedric Player was just a stage actor on the eve of appearing in his first silent one-reeler. But for as much as the place gave me a curious peace of mind, I didn't belong here and I didn't think Kimberly Eames belonged here. I associated her with a Manhattan residential tower, a spacious apartment with large windows that overlooked the East River and the south skyline of the city. The Gardens had charm; Manhattan had vitality.

I became aware of piano music half a block away on Greenway South. It was a Rachmaninoff piece, the "Romance in F Sharp Minor." It was beautifully played, and I followed the music until I came to Number 29.

Last time I had heard Schumann. Now this. Both were played with the confident, professional skill that allowed a musician room for interpretation. I opened the gate, quietly shut it behind me, and went up the flagstone steps to the porch. Through a window I could see a black grand piano in the far corner of a large room. The player was focused on her work. I sat on the steps and listened. It could carry me along for a day or two before I would want to do anything else.

Then there was something that started angry and ended sublime and when she stopped, I rang the bell.

"How long were you out there?" Kimberly Eames asked.

"Long enough."

We were in the kitchen, waiting on coffee, and for the moment I wasn't interested in the questions I had come to ask. "You trained for a music career?" I said.

"From the age of four. My parents wanted it and so did I. I loved music, loved learning to play it."

"The last piece . . . 'Dies Irae,'" I said, "from Mozart's 'Requiem.' I didn't know there was a piano transcription of it."

"Not in any catalogue," said Kimberly. "My piano instructor wrote it for me when I was twelve, to practice with. He said that when I could play it to his satisfaction, then I'd be a pianist and ready for a music career."

"Did you ever play it to your teacher's satisfaction?"

"Once," sighed Kimberly. "I was eighteen. I played it for him, and then told him that I didn't want a music career. By then I'd appeared in some plays in high school, and was drawn to acting—because of music. I wanted to convey something that music could complement, or underscore, or dramatize. He understood. He died a few years later and left me the rights to the transcription. I'm the only student of his to have played it."

"What made you play it a while ago?"

"An urge to stand up, to lift myself out of the grayness I'd let collect around me. To talk to myself." She looked at me. "Why did you come here, Chess?"

"To ask you to let me see Munro's screenplay, the one he *did* write, and dedicated to his best friend at school, Patrick Player."

I thought the words might jar her, but they didn't. She said, "Come with me." She led me down the hallway.

The study was almost as large as the living room and held about twice the number of books on its floor-to-ceiling shelves. There were two desks, with a leather armchair at one and a plain office chair at the other. What little exposed wall space was left by the bookcases held pictures and photographs, some of the subjects of Munro's biographies, some of men presumably his colleagues. There were a few of Munro at various stages of his life, including one of him and Kimberly atop the Empire State Building, and one of him and Player in a Vickers Prep play production I couldn't identify.

The largest item was a framed movie poster for the original *Swift Sword*. Kimberly went to an old wooden file cabinet, opened one of the drawers, and took out an envelope. She opened it, extracted a bound sheaf of papers, and handed it to me. "This is what you came for."

It was a carbon copy of *The Stars Within*, also on onionskin paper. "Yes," I said.

We walked through the neighborhood and down to Queens Boulevard. There was a six-screen movie theater nearby, its marquee offering nothing I wanted to see. We entered a café, sat at a table by the window. Kimberly was quiet for a while. Then she said, "I never wanted to be a comedienne. How can a joker or a buffoon value *anything*? And if he could, why should anyone take him seriously?" She glanced at me. "I've told myself these last few years that I quit acting because the kinds of scripts I wanted weren't being written or produced. But if they were, who would offer them to *me*—after *Falling Bodies*?"

Anyone might, I thought. But I said, "I had a long talk with Player last night. Munro was his chief target with the screenplay credit. You were just icing on the cake. He volunteered everything."

"I suppose he couldn't refuse you answers, either."

I shrugged. "I think it was more his wanting to boast about what he'd done to Munro and the screenplay. Were there offers to you after *Falling Bodies*?"

"For a while, yes, mostly for low grade farces. I refused to acknowledge them. Then they stopped coming." Kimberly paused. "I'm surprised you were able to get to him," she said. "Patrick Player, I mean. He admitted everything?"

I nodded. "Even his motive. As punishment for me. For some people, truth-telling is a form of malice, when they think they're beyond justice." I told Kimberly about my two encounters with Player. "I was expecting to hear something a little more involved, such as how Munro might have hurt him in the past. Munro did hurt him, though not in the usual way." I shook my head in amazement. "Listen to this, Kimberly: If anyone else had written that exact same letter in the *Times*, Player wouldn't have cared. He'd have dismissed it and the correspondence that followed it and the *Observer* article and just never minded what anyone else might have said about him or his career or the picture.

"But your husband had known Player. The letter was a personal reproach to him. Player couldn't let the contrast stand—the contrast between himself and Munro, and the contrast between himself and what he'd been years ago. So he struck back the only way he could. That's all there was to it." I paused. "Has anyone else ever questioned the authorship of the screenplay Player used?"

"No," said Kimberly, "not that I know of."

"I'm the first outsider?"

"I suppose you have that distinction."

"Did either of you ever consider a lawsuit over *Falling Bodies*?"

"Forbes did, before we met. But his attorney advised against it, since Forbes had indeed sold the script to Player's father, as well as all the rights to its dramatic use. Even if a court agreed with the wrongness of what Player did to Forbes's script, the suit would have to be thrown out on grounds of the privilege of 'artistic license.'"

Kimberly paused. "Myself? I signed a contract to appear in that picture. I was led to believe it would be a drama, not a farce. I was given a script to read—it had Forbes's name on it, as the author—and I even bought a copy of Forbes's biography of Galileo, which I was told was the basis of the script. I was very excited about it, by the script, by the chance to appear in a production with some of my favorite actors—by everything that was happening. So I signed the contract."

"And all your scenes were shot separately from the others?"

"Yes, but I thought nothing of it all through production. I'd just assumed that was the best shooting schedule they could arrange. And during production, I grew intrigued by Forbes Munro. I read several of his other books—most of them—during that time. They simply assured me that I was doing the right thing. His name was on the script. Why should I suspect anything? Soquel shot all my scenes as they'd been printed and made hardly any changes. It was going to be a great picture, a great story, and I had a key role. I was happy. I even began to think better of Patrick Player, whom I did not like personally and whose career I'd never intended to be a model for my own."

"Didn't you know what they'd done before the picture was released?"

Kimberly shook her head. "No. It was edited right up to the last moment, a few days before it opened in the theaters. That's a common practice. No one who appeared in it was able to see it from start to finish, not until it had been released. I might have insisted on it, but I was getting offers to appear in other pictures and I was busy reading new scripts my agent sent me and negotiating with other producers."

"And then you saw *Falling Bodies*."

"Yes." Kimberly became quiet. "I even paid for a ticket to see how my career had been ruined. In a midtown theater. It was defilement, Chess. The same kind of defilement you must have felt when you saw it for the first time, but ten times worse, because that was *me* up there. That's what I felt, when I saw it at last, after they'd edited it and added the score and released it for millions of people to see. I'd had a hand in it, and I can't think of it without feeling duped, and ashamed and humiliated. And anger, but—you know what happened to the anger. It's what Forbes felt, too, I learned later. How could I sue Player, or Autumn Harvest, or Twin Dolphins, Chess? On what grounds? I signed a contract, and I delivered."

"But didn't you suspect something when you learned that Player and his Autumn Harvest company were behind it? After all, he did the remake of *Swift Sword* and two comedies before *Falling Bodies*."

"Of course I was suspicious. At first. But it was the script he sent me through the agent. That was what convinced me. There wasn't any room in it for improvisation, or for altering the story or the balance of the characters or scenes or anything like that. It was a script ready for a director to shoot from. And I'd have signed a contract for much less money and worse terms, because there was that script, and the chance to work with Dean Tolland and Allan Swain and Kit Aragon. These are . . . were great actors. They'd appeared in so little for so long, simply because they were greater than the material that was being written, no one could fit them into pygmy stories and roles. So I reasoned that if *they* had decided to appear in that picture, then it must have been because they thought the script was worth it. I thought it was because Player respected their stature too much to try and pull one of his slimy stunts. And last and first, there was the script. . . ."

"You were lied to."

Kimberly nodded. "And I was wrong about Tolland and the others. They'd stopped caring about what they did. They were asked to do caricatures of themselves. You saw it. It takes great skill to caricature oneself, Chess. They did a splendid job. They didn't have to fool everyone. Just me." The anger in her eyes abruptly turned inward.

I said, "I have more questions, Kimberly. I want to set this thing straight in my mind once and for all."

"Of course. Ask me anything."

"Munro's original screenplay—the one he wrote at Vickers—did it bear any resemblance to the one you worked with in the picture?'

"Yes. The best of everything in Forbes's was in the one Player sent me. I still have a copy of that. Forbes showed me everything in it that Player had lifted." Kimberly smiled. "When you read Forbes's script, you'll see that there wasn't even a part in it for me. I played Teresa Cinthio, Cardinal Bellarmine's mistress. She had some of the best lines. Forbes didn't write them."

"Then Player did," I said. "And he apparently wrote two screenplays: the one he sent you—as a lure—and the one he and Soquel actually used."

Kimberly studied her coffee. "Forbes and I speculated that Player might have done that. But we couldn't believe it." She paused, then said, in the manner of a quotation, "Courage isn't the same as bravado. Valor isn't synonymous with suffering. And justice has little to do with penance. They're not in the same moral equation." She looked at me. "I said those lines in *Falling Bodies*, Chess. And Player must have written them. Or someone who worked for him wrote them. Did you see that scene?"

I shook my head. "No. I left the theater about a third of the way into the picture."

"Teresa spoke the words to Cardinal Bellarmine, after she learned he would not speak out in defense of Galileo, and before she left him. It was a wonderful scene, Chess."

"Did Player say anything to you after the picture came out?"

"I never saw or heard from him again. I tried to see him—to demand an explanation—but he was already busy with his next picture and never in town. It was impossible to get him on the phone or to find out where he was. I'd been to both his homes, the one in Beverly Hills and the one up in Westchester, to rehearse some scenes with him and Tolland, but he must have told his servants and staff never to admit he was around. I wrote him through his agent and Twin Dolphins and Autumn Harvest, but never got a reply. I had to give up. I think he knew I would."

"How did you and Munro meet?"

"Forbes wanted an explanation, too, and got the same run-around. He learned the name of my agent, and a meeting was arranged between us. In the beginning, we were both angry with each other. He with me because he liked me as an actress and it had pained him to see me in that picture, and I with him, because I thought he'd doctored his own script over and over again to suit Player or Soquel. Then we learned how we'd been used, and when our anger was gone, we were left with ourselves." Kimberly mused, "But we were both affected by the experience, Chess. You know how I felt. Forbes tried to help me come out of it, and I did, a little, but not entirely. I don't think he knew how to help me. He was in something of the same kind of trap. He became obsessed with paying back Player somehow, if only for the record."

"How?" I asked. "What could he do?"

"He began researching a history of the Player family."

I frowned. "Why would he bother with that?"

"He said he wanted to exonerate the rest of the family by writing their stories, to demonstrate Patrick Player's true stature by comparing him with his father, grandfather, and even his great-grandfather, to show how much had been betrayed. He started work on it about a year after we were married. I wasn't very enthusiastic about it. I haven't read what he finished of the book."

I vaguely recalled something Professor Downey said when I talked with him at Ploughsmith College. I shook my head in confusion. "But how could he write such a book without Player's cooperation? He'd have to use the family archives, if they exist, and to be able to talk with Player himself, and to people Player associated with in and out of the industry. Player wouldn't have given him the time of day, and neither would any of his friends, if he told them not to. Player's too rich a gravy train."

Kimberly made a face. "He had some help. Forbes was a

professional researcher and he made more progress than you might imagine. For one thing, he was already familiar with Player's family history. He had visited Soundview when he and Player were friends. And a dozen biographies had already been written on the family since the turn of the century, and he'd arranged to get access to those authors' notes and material. And there were countless interviews and articles about each of the Players that had never been collected in one book. Somehow he'd managed to contact a few of Player's colleagues, actors and actresses who were disgruntled for one reason or another, and he got some information from them."

Kimberly paused to search her memory. "And one day, about two and a half years ago, even Elliott Rhodes came forward and volunteered to talk about Player. Or was it three? Well, Forbes sent him a letter, which just said that he would like to speak to him, but it was never answered. About a year later, Rhodes showed up at Ploughsmith College and saw Forbes there." She frowned and leaned back in her chair. "I didn't like the idea. I'd never liked Rhodes. I made the only demand on my husband ever: that he never let Rhodes into our home. They met near the college or at Rhodes's apartment in Manhattan. Rhodes was a friend of Player's. He was able to get into the family archives at Soundview and to talk to Player's other friends and associates without letting them know he was collecting information for Forbes."

I sat back in my chair, too. "Why would Rhodes do that?"

Kimberly shrugged. "I'd heard that Rhodes was originally cast in the role of Cardinal Bellarmine in *Falling Bodies*, but Dean Tolland got it instead because of some conflict of favors between Soquel and Player. I supposed Rhodes carried a grudge against Player for not fighting harder for him. The picture was a commercial success and could have resurrected Rhodes's career. I don't know if Rhodes is even still acting now." She sighed. "It's just speculation on my part, Chess. I don't know what Rhodes's reasons were. I didn't trust him, and neither did Forbes. He might have been reporting back to Player on what Forbes was up to."

I said, "And your husband never got to finish the family history?"

"No. He abandoned it. For all the material he was able to collect by himself and from Rhodes and the other sources, he wasn't satisfied that he had enough to write a reputable history. He couldn't research it as thoroughly as he'd have liked to, and he didn't like having to rely on Rhodes and all the secondary sources he'd managed to put together. He came into the living room one evening last March and told me he'd dropped the project. He was tired and discouraged. He said he wasn't interested in writing what he called a 'grudge biography.' He never mentioned it again."

An idea was beginning to form in my mind. "May I see it, Kimberly?"

"His first draft wasn't finished. It's mostly a mass of papers and a couple of notebooks. Why would you want to see it?"

"Curiosity," I said. I didn't want her to know what I was thinking. "You see, I talked with Rhodes last night, too. He used to be a hero of mine. So was Player, once." Her eyes were watchful. I said, "Kimberly, what had you planned to do eventually?"

She toyed with her empty coffee cup. "Get over my problems enough to where I could think clearly. Probably sell the house and move away from this area. The income from my other pictures—not including *Falling Bodies*, which I've never counted—is large enough to keep me if I choose not to do anything. And there's the income from Forbes's books, which never seem to stop going into new printings. I still have my agent, and I still get offers."

"Hollywood hasn't changed," I suggested.

"I'd be cautious, very cautious."

She would have to be, I thought, but it might not be enough. They wouldn't want cautious talent. Carelessness was the watchword, the operative ethic. Conscientious, premeditated carelessness.

Chapter 20

"It's gone."

"What's gone?"

Kimberly stood staring into one of the open drawers of the wooden file cabinet in Munro's study. I was leafing through the slick pages of his screenplay. She said, "The folder—a big brown cardboard folder with all of Forbes's notes and correspondence and his typewritten outline—it's not here."

I put down the script and went over. The drawer was thickly packed with files in folders that hung from runners on the sides. Kimberly pointed to a space in between the folders with tabs marked "Oxford Correspondence" and "Ploughsmith Papers." I had the same kind of folders in my office cabinet. I stooped down and separated the Oxford and Ploughsmith folders. Sometimes a folder would be knocked off the tracks and slip to the bottom. But there was nothing down there but dust.

"How was the folder marked?" I asked as I stood up.

"Player Bio," said Kimberly.

"And you're certain it was in this drawer?"

"Yes."

"Let's make sure."

Together we checked the three remaining drawers. Unless the papers had been stuffed into another folder, they weren't in the cabinet.

"Could the folder be anywhere else?"

"No."

"When was the last time you saw it?"

"Last May, when I went through everything of Forbes's here with our attorney. No, I saw it again, when Forbes's agent came to see me. I showed him the notes Forbes had compiled for a biography of Newton, and we settled a contract for his last collection of essays, and I showed him that file, the one on the Player family, but he wasn't interested. I mean, he was interested, but just curious, and he didn't want to represent it."

"Albert Lundy, of Friendship and Room?"

"Yes."

"And you haven't opened these drawers since?"

"Yes, I have. Occasionally letters have come from historians and other biographers, from people who didn't know Forbes had died. I've answered them and filed them away in one of the folders. And then I'm always getting royalty checks and statements from his publisher, but all his book business is in folders in the desk drawer, here." Kimberly went over to the smaller desk and slid out one of the side drawers.

"Let's check both desks," I said.

We did. And found nothing.

"You're certain it couldn't be anywhere else in this house?"

"I'm certain."

I went over and glanced at the French doors and windows. There were no signs of a forced entry. The lock on the door looked as though it hadn't been used in a long while. The bolts that secured the windows were thick with dust.

"What are you doing?" Kimberly asked.

"Has this house ever been broken into?"

"No."

I shook my head. "That you know of. I want to see the rest of the house. Is there an alarm hooked to the local precinct or a security agency?"

"Yes. But I often forget to switch it on. I shouldn't, but I do."

I looked over the system. Every window and exterior door was wired. The front door had three locks: two standard pickproof locks and another that deactivated the alarm system. Kimberly said that she rarely used the key to the third lock.

I asked, "Did your husband keep an appointment book?"

I followed her back to the study. There were no appointment books on either desk. "There was one!" she said. "One of those red leather ones. I remember checking it shortly after Forbes died. He'd had meetings and things to do marked months ahead. . . ."

"Do you remember notes for his meetings with Rhodes?"

"Yes, and some others. There were three or four of them early this year. Whether he actually met Rhodes on those dates, I couldn't say. He was also seeing people who had worked with Player on the stage or in pictures." She mentioned several names that meant nothing to me.

"Did your husband tell Rhodes or the others he was shelving the book?"

She shook her head. "I'm sorry, I don't know."

A number of people could have wanted to get to Munro's notes and appointments list. Sources Munro or Rhodes recruited could have had second thoughts. But that was reaching, and I didn't think I needed to reach.

We had another coffee. I asked, "What did you do to Player that he wanted to get back at you?"

"Nothing, except I had to tell him I didn't want anything but a professional relationship with him."

"Your 'nothing' must have been 'something' to him."

At the door I reminded her to turn on the alarm system. I headed back for the city.

Two incidents. Munro's murder in April, and the subsequent theft of his notes and appointment book. They didn't have to be connected. If they were . . .

In theory, either Player or Rhodes could have murdered Forbes Munro in Central Park. Whether they could have done so in fact was another matter. I didn't know where either man had been on that night in April. I could make similar thin arguments for a number of people in Munro's orbit. But for the moment I stuck with Player. If the actor had done it, then most likely it was because he'd learned of Munro's biographical project and wanted to block it. But how plausible was that?

Not very.

First, Player had already done his damage. He was satisfied. Second, he seemed to care little for what the public thought of him. Third, anything Munro wrote would be discredited in advance by his association with *Falling Bodies*. Fourth, had Player even known about Munro's work-in-progress?

Then again, Player had remarked to me last night that what he'd done to Munro's name was more satisfying than murder. How would *he* know?

It had been a careless remark. No, I corrected myself: It had been an innocent remark. Patrick Player didn't make careless remarks. From the moment we'd met, he'd demonstrated self-control. He was a man of carefully considered words and actions.

So was Elliott Rhodes, who might have a motive for wanting Munro silenced: his renewed association with Player, his starring role in Player's latest project, *The Thankful Corpse*. But was that a strong enough motive for murder? It depended on something I didn't know—just what Rhodes might have told Forbes Munro. In theory—back to that—he could have said something so dreadful that Player would use all his considerable influence to bury Rhodes's career once again.

Without Munro's notes, I wasn't going to find out. Rhodes wouldn't let on. He was as good an actor as Player.

I tried to build a plausible scenario: Rhodes so stung by being passed over for *Falling Bodies* that he strikes back. He cultivates

Player's friendship and feeds tidbits to a man he senses bears a deeper grudge. Then he lands a plum role and tries to cover up.

Rhodes *had* expressed interest in the chance that *I* might write a book about Player.

My thinking went on like that, round and round, all the way back to Manhattan. It was nearly three o'clock when I turned onto Park Avenue. I lucked out and found a parking spot only two blocks from my office. When I'd sat at the desk for five minutes, I called Kimberly.

"Can you remember the exact date Forbes told you that he'd quit the Player history?"

"I think so. It was the day when Mr. Lundy, Forbes's agent, called him at school to tell him his publisher was willing to sign a contract for two more biographies. And some faculty members threw a party that afternoon to mark his fifteenth anniversary at Ploughsmith . . . a Thursday, just before the last weekend of March."

I looked at my own calendar. The last weekend of the month. The previous Thursday was the 23rd. I remembered that date, too. I was packing for my trip to Europe and hoping Walker wouldn't go on a hunger strike in the kennel.

Next I called Ellen Romero at the *Chronicle*. "You again?" she said.

"Me again, Ellen. Write your Soundview column yet?"

"Put the last juicy period in it about an hour ago. Why do you ask?"

"Last night you mentioned Player's new picture, the *Corpse* thing. Do you recall when and where you saw the announcement about the casting? Was it in *Variety*?"

"No doubt it was reported in *Variety*, Chess," she said. "But I saw it in the *Chronicle*, in Bill Yount's 'Take Five' column. Why?"

I chuckled. "I don't know why yet, Ellen. Would you dig it up and read it to me if it's short? I'm pressed for time."

"Have you forgotten your promise?"

"What do you think I'm working on?"

"All right, sleuth. I'll call you back in a few minutes. Bill's already left for the day, which means I'll have to haul out some back issues."

I replaced the receiver and lit a cigarette, then swung around in my chair to look out the window and wait. A shaft of sunlight broke through the cloud ceiling over in Jersey and traced a path over the land like a giant searchlight. I reached back for a pen and notepad and wrote "March 23." Then I dropped the pen and leaned back to think of Kimberly.

The phone rang once and I had the receiver pressed to my ear before the second ring.

"All right, here we are," Romero said, "from 'Take Five,' March 31st edition. Yount wrote: 'Patrick Player will team again with Elliott Rhodes in a Twin Dolphins-Autumn Harvest co-production of Richard Welling's *The Thankful Corpse*, to begin shooting late in December. Selby Lane, veteran character actor, and Tilley Lace, the teen actress who put the "Gee!" in *ingénue*, will also star. Welling, cult figure of neo-*noir* fiction, and author of the hyper-bizarre "non-murder mystery," a runaway bestseller, is nearing completion of the script. George Soquel will direct under producers Sproule and Grunnian. Rhodes, slated to portray the monomaniacal Tom Turlock to Player's ghostly, bonbon-popping mobster, Pluennkey, signed a three-picture contract last week with Autumn Harvest, of which this will be the first.' That's it, Chess."

"Three pictures, eh?" I mused.

"You have a special interest in Rhodes?"

"I'll admit that much, but that's all for now. I'll talk to you soon." I put the received back.

Three pictures. *That* was motive enough, I thought. My "plausible scenario" about Rhodes looked better.

I pulled the phone over again and dialed my moody friend at the Midtown East precinct, Lieutenant James Navarro. A sergeant told me he was out. Then abruptly Navarro answered. "Navarro here."

"It's me, James. May I pop up?"

"No. I'm busy on a case."

"I've got a lead on the Munro murder. I need to see your file."

"I would mind that a hell of a lot, Chess. It would mean my having to talk to you about it again, and listen to your book talk, and I don't have the time."

"If you let me see the file, I'll invite you to dinner with Kimberly Eames."

Something like doubt was transmitted silently through the wires. Then Navarro said, "Come on up."

Chapter 21

In Navarro's office, after I'd filled him in on what I'd discovered over the last few days, I looked over the original and subsequent reports, the first written by a Sergeant Carmoody, who'd since transferred to a downtown precinct, said Navarro, and Navarro's own regulation "progress" report, which he'd filed three months ago after having made no progress.

Munro was murdered the night of April 5th, a Wednesday, some time between ten o'clock and midnight. His body was found on a path beneath a foot bridge by two mounted officers the next morning. He was murdered exactly two weeks after he'd told Kimberly that he was abandoning the Player history, and two days short of a week after news of Player's latest project was reported in the papers. Navarro's reports confirmed what he'd told me a week ago. Munro's effects were taken by someone—probably the killer—and discarded randomly in the bushes and grass along the path leading back to Fifth Avenue.

Among the other forms with the reports was one with a list of the personal effects returned to his widow, and signed by her on receipt. Everything had been recovered, except the cash from Munro's wallet, and his keys. Everything included the wallet with identification and credit cards, two books on loan from the Forest Hills and Ploughsmith College libraries, a notebook, some pens and pencils, a palm-sized calculator, a phone, a copy of the speech Munro had delivered that evening at the conference, a personal address book, and the briefcase that held most of those things. The search had turned up stray keys in the vicinity, but none of them Munro's.

I glanced at Navarro, who sat watching me quietly. I dug out my phone and called Kimberly. "Business again. Your husband's keys were never returned to you, were they?"

"Now that you mention it, no. I think I asked about them at the time, but the police assumed they were lost. Why?"

"I'm calling from the police station. I have the report in my hand. How did he carry his keys?"

"In a leather case I bought him for his birthday. He kept all his keys in it—to the house, his office at school, his car." Kimberly paused. "I see what you're thinking."

"How often did you leave the house after he died?"

"I was away the longest when I visited my parents in Chicago for a few days—that was later in April. And in May I was gone for a week or so to drive up through New England. That was after I met with our attorney and Mr. Lundy. And of course I go for long walks almost every day, aside from going out to shop and do other errands."

He'd been a very patient burglar, I thought. He'd waited until there was no chance of encountering Kimberly in or near the house. I asked, "Did your husband ever use the third key to the front door, the alarm key?"

"Yes, he'd set the alarm whenever we went out. So did I when I went to New England and Chicago." Her phone was in the living room and I heard a car go up Greenway through her open window. Kimberly said, "He must have been watching me, Chess. For over a month."

"Yes, he must have," I answered, and did not voice my other

thoughts. He could have killed Kimberly just as easily as he'd killed her husband, but two murders in the family might have tipped off the police to look a little more closely into Munro's life. "Well, that's over now. Don't think about it. I'll call later."

I pocketed the phone, asked Navarro, "What about Munro's hotel key? The conference was at Tivoli Towers, but he was staying at the Doncaster, it says here."

"We checked," said Navarro. "It's there in the report. He left the room key at the front desk. His room was made up after he left for the conference. It hadn't been touched since. The Doncaster is a budget-priced tourist hotel, quaint but with minimal amenities."

"Okay," I said, closing the folder and setting it on the desk.

Navarro said, "So you think Munro's house was burglarized by the killer. . . ."

"The discarded briefcase and books were a ruse," I said. "So was the way Munro was killed, with the smashed skull and broken ribs. It looked as though a psychotic had attacked him. You thought so, I thought so. If it weren't for the burglary and the missing files and datebook, I might still think so. But the killer didn't bother to keep anything with Munro's address on it, did he? Nothing that would tell him where the professor lived. Just the keys."

Navarro nodded. "Because the killer didn't need the address." He tapped a finger on his desk. "Player or Rhodes?"

"My bet."

"What do you propose to do about it? It's been almost eight months. Whoever did it will have an alibi. The physical evidence—those book notes of Munro's—must have been destroyed." He paused for another sip of coffee. "What about Eames? Can she give us a reason to question Rhodes? Did she meet him during that time, see him before or after the murder?"

I shook my head. "She hasn't seen Rhodes since they worked on a picture together years ago."

"*Someone* must have seen Munro and Rhodes together."

"Sure," I said. "Skillions of people probably did. But where?

How many times? How long ago? And why would they remember? Kimberly said that Munro met Rhodes at his office at Ploughsmith, but it was probably after hours."

Navarro said, "What you've got is pounds of speculation but not an ounce of evidence."

"I know. I haven't been in that part of Central Park in a while. Is it safe to walk through at the time of night Munro was killed?"

"Safe enough, if you're not alone. Foolhardy, otherwise."

"So do we assume Munro was alone, or that he had a companion?"

"We can assume anything we like," Navarro said. "If I take this downtown, they'll say we couldn't even legitimately ask Rhodes where he was on the night of the murder. We don't have enough to view him as a suspect. And Player—even less."

"Well, I'll work on it," I said.

If it was Rhodes, he must have breathed easier as months passed and he saw that he'd done the right things to fool everybody.

That comfort would have ended last night at Player's post-banquet party when he met me.

I walked up Fifth Avenue toward Central Park, trying to remember the little things that belonged in the puzzle. I toyed with the idea Munro might have abandoned his book because Rhodes, fresh from signing the three-picture contract with Autumn Harvest, had pulled out. But Munro would have told Kimberly of that setback, and he hadn't mentioned it. Also, Kimberly had remarked that she didn't know whether Rhodes was still acting. Which meant that neither she nor Munro knew about the new films. Turning it around, I wondered if Munro had told Rhodes the book project was dead. If so, it hadn't saved his life.

Rhodes had wiped out most of the evidence of his relationship with Munro. Time had blurred everything else. Except for my appearance, he would feel safe. He could try to fix that situation, which I sort of hoped he would do. I would be waiting for him.

Or . . . he could decide that Kimberly had to go.

I got to the Park. The workday was nearly over and people on foot were cutting through it on their way to the other side of town. I found the scene of Munro's murder, the little asphalt path that passed under a stone foot bridge. There was nothing to see now except how easy it must have been to kill a man in this place.

Half way back to my office building, something popped into my mind like the price on one of those old-fashioned cash registers: Cynthia Vogel, the frumpy dean's secretary at Ploughsmith College. I thought of her because I remembered Kimberly had said Rhodes had turned up at Ploughsmith one day to offer Munro his help. Cynthia Vogel might have given him the same directions she'd given me to Beal Hall. And she might remember his face. It was four-thirty. I phoned as I walked faster. She still might be at her desk.

The line for the dean's office was busy. I tried again.

By the time I reached my office, the busy signal was gone and the line rang but nobody picked up. With one hand holding the phone to my ear I struggled out of my raincoat. Finally, after eleven rings, someone answered. A brusque male voice said, "Ploughsmith College."

"May I speak with Cynthia Vogel, please, if she hasn't gone home yet."

He said, "Mrs. Vogel had an accident and can't talk. Call back tomorrow."

"An accident? What happened?"

"Not now, please. Tomorrow." He broke the connection.

I looked around for one of the movie picture books I'd bought, but I'd taken them all home. I had planned to take a book that had recent photos of Player and Rhodes to the college and ask Vogel if she'd ever seen either man in her office.

Two messages were waiting for me on the answering machine, but I called Kimberly first.

"I want to clear a couple of things up in my mind," I said, "and then I'm going to ask you to stay at my place tonight. How soon after Forbes's death was his office at Ploughsmith cleaned out?"

"About two weeks after the funeral. I did it myself, with the help of a colleague of his, Professor Downey."

"Had the office been searched?"

"I don't know. It never occurred to me. Forbes didn't keep things as neat there as he did at home."

"Do you know where Rhodes lives?" I asked her.

"He used to have an apartment on East Fifty-third, near Second Avenue. And a place out in Santa Monica. I went to both for readings with others in the cast of *Fraction of Fear* during pre-production. . . . Why?"

"I might pay him a visit."

"Chess," Kimberly said, "why don't you leave that to the police?"

"I will, when there's something to leave them. I'm going to pick you up later. Pack enough for a weekend. All right?"

"All right."

"You aren't allergic to cats, are you?"

"No. Why?"

"I have one. He's quiet, discreet, and a model of good behavior."

I tried the dean's office at Ploughsmith once more, but after fifteen rings I gave up. I listened to my waiting messages. The first was from Robert Downey, Munro's colleague at the college. "Mr. Hanrahan," the professor said, "this is Robert Downey. It's two-thirty. I just wanted to tell you I finally remembered what else I wanted to tell you during your visit the other day. It might be important, and it might not. You be the judge. Call me here or at home this evening." He recited his office and home numbers.

As I wrote the numbers down on a pad, the second message started. "Mr. Hanrahan, it's about three-forty-five and this is Detective Sergeant Kershaw of the Queens Village precinct. As soon as possible could you please call me or Detective Sergeant Aaron here at this number?" Kershaw rattled off his number. "We have some questions for you. Better still, we'd appreciate it if you came out our way." Then he recited an address, but I didn't take it down because I knew where that station was. "We just want to ask you some questions."

The Queens Village station was right down the hill from Ploughsmith College. I'd passed it. It was only a block away from the florist's shop where I'd ordered a vase of roses for Cynthia Vogel.

Chapter 22

"*She never came back from lunch. Around* two o'clock someone in one of the offices on her floor dropped a flask of coffee in the hall and went to the janitor's sink room for a mop. There she was, in her coat and hat, sitting on the floor, propped against the wall. Her wrists were slashed, and she was dead. That's what was used."

Sergeant Kershaw indicated the bottom half a blue glass vase I'd had the florist's shop send the roses in. The remnant was intact and sat atop his desk in the Queens Village station. The other half, in a hundred tiny pieces, sat next to it in a plastic bag. There were dried blood stains on some of the jagged points of the intact half.

Allan Kershaw was a tall, almost cadaverous man with bitter, impatient eyes. He was nearing retirement age and a pension and he seemed to resent the imposition of his job. Eric Aaron, his partner, sat quietly near a file cabinet and said little. He was Kershaw's junior by a generation and would soon need a stint with Weight Watchers. He didn't look very concerned, either.

I said, "So, you don't think she slashed her own wrists."

"Why might I not think that, Mr. Hanrahan?" Kershaw asked.

"Because you implied it."

Kershaw smiled. "If we'd found her at home like that, we wouldn't have thought twice about it. As it was, we did think twice. They make it so easy for us. Her boss, the Dean, said she'd been as chipper as a chipmunk all week, and the last time he saw her alive was when she went to get rid of the wilted roses you sent her and wash out the vase. She still had your card from the florist's. Found it in her desk. That's why we called you." Kershaw opened a folder and took out the card I'd written. He held it up and read it out loud. "'Thanks for your help. Here's something for *your* eyes.'" He put the card back inside the folder. "What did you mean by that, Mr. Hanrahan?"

I gave him a synopsis of my conversation with Cynthia Vogel on Monday.

"That's all?" Kershaw asked, frowning.

"That's all," I said. "Let's keep to the subject. You suspect a homicide. So do I. Let's trade reasons."

Kershaw shrugged. "That's none of your business, whether we do or not."

"Wrong. It is my business. If you don't believe that, call Lieutenant James Navarro at Midtown East. There might be a link between Vogel's murder and a Central Park murder from April. He might be generous enough to share the credit if and when he establishes the link."

Kershaw rose from his chair. "I'm through with you, so you can leave. Eric, escort the gentleman out of the building."

I shrugged, stood up, touched my hat, and left. Sergeant Aaron walked me to the door downstairs. "What's his problem?" I asked.

"He doesn't like private investigators. One got the goods on him for his ex-wife. He's still paying half his salary in alimony."

"Why do *you* suspect a homicide?" I asked. "Or do you have an ex-wife?"

"The M.E. found a little bump on her neck, just below the right ear. She might've been knocked unconscious and put into that closet. Or someone snuck up on her while she was washing the vase. Something like that. The strap on her purse was broken. The purse was beneath the sink. There were drag marks on the heels of her nylons, they picked up dirt. Her blouse had ridden up and became untucked from her skirt. And she was still wearing her wristwatch, for Christ's sake. And we found pieces of the vase outside the closet, in the hallway, as though whoever did it smashed the vase inside and particles of it wedged in his shoes and dropped off as he left the building."

"That's good detail work," I said.

"Were you serious about that link you mentioned?"

I nodded. "Talk with Navarro. He'll fill you in."

"We will." We were standing outside the station now. Aaron said, "You know, she kept those roses beyond the wilting point. She threw all of them out but one. It was in her purse, wrapped in cellophane. The Dean—her boss—said she'd told him she was taking the vase home. She lived only two blocks from here. Usually went there for lunch."

"Then the killer didn't know that. He could've followed her home and saved himself the risk. But—he was in a hurry." I was thinking out loud. "And I guess no one else at the school noticed anything."

"No one," said Aaron. "Classes were in session, teachers at their podiums, and no one else was roaming the hall. That's when Vogel usually took her lunch." He paused. "Any ideas?"

"Just one," I said. "She could recognize him." I paused. "Ask Navarro for details." I touched my hat again and went my way.

I phoned Kimberly. "I'll be there in a bit. Make sure your door is locked."

Then I thought: *He has a key.*

"Bolt it from the inside," I said.

As I drove I tried to convince myself he had no need to

eliminate Kimberly. She hadn't seen him and her husband together. Couldn't prove anything. . . .

I stepped on the gas anyway.

She opened the door before I could press the bell.

She hugged me and then saw my face. "What's wrong?"

We went inside and I told her about Cynthia Vogel. "She was probably the only person at the school who might remember Rhodes's visit. She paid attention to faces. He decided he couldn't risk it. I'm worried he'll decide the same about you."

"Couldn't there be another reason the woman was killed?"

"Not at the school, not that way. Not so soon after I talked to Rhodes and Player.It was a clumsy job, done in haste. Almost panic. Are you packed?"

Kimberly smiled. "What's your cat's name?"

"Walker. He attached himself to me as a kitten years ago. He has blue-gray eyes, deep orange fur, and your legs."

She laughed. "Well, I'm sure I'm flattered."

"Wait until you see him." I moved uneasily toward her husband's study. "I've got to call Navarro. And Professor Downey. Do you want to get a coat?"

Navarro had gone home, a sergeant told me. I fished around for the slip of paper I'd written Robert Downey's number on.

"Chess," said Kimberly.

I walked out of the study. She was standing by the door to a coat closet. Beside her stood Elliott Rhodes. He stared back at me with sad eyes. Kimberly's were ovals of fear. The actor raised a gun—a Mauser—so that I could see it.

"Come slowly," he said.

I stood still.

He said, "I can shoot her here, and you where you stand."

"Why don't you?"

"Because I know you wouldn't want her to die so uselessly, and because I know you're itching to do something."

I walked down the hall. Rhodes put a hand on Kimberly's

shoulder and pulled her away with the gun still pointed at her back.

"How much do you think I know?" I asked.

"Too much, Mr. Hanrahan. I let myself in an hour ago. I was going to take care of my business, but then you called. I thought I'd wait for you." Rhodes shook his head. "Interesting greeting she gave you. I stood in the hallway upstairs while you explained some of it to her. Then I knew I was right to be here."

He was wearing a clearance sale raincoat, a driving cap with sunglasses resting on the bill, gray trousers, rubber-soled shoes.

I said, "If I know too much, then so do the police."

Rhodes shook his head again. "If the police knew too much, they would have come with you. Or I would have heard from them. And even if they credit your suspicions, there's no proof left for them to act on. Absolutely none. And I can't afford to be as generous as Patrick and offer you or anyone else a brazen confession. *His* crimes are not statutory. You said so yourself, last night."

He was wrong about there being no proof.

Rhodes said, "There is a door beneath the stairs behind you, Mr. Hanrahan. It leads to the basement. Please go to it, open it, and turn on the basement lights just inside the door."

I turned and obliged him as slowly as I dared. "What tipped you off, Rhodes?"

"Nothing in particular," he said from behind me. "Just your intellect. The way you dealt with Patrick. And with me. The moral outrage of your esthetic sensibilities. I sensed that if the question of this dear lady's husband's death did not occur to you last night, it soon would. I was right. So very right."

I turned. "You know, you never checked to see if I was wearing a gun."

"I know you're not wearing one. I've had to don too many shoulder holsters in my career not to be able to spot one."

I put on a thoughtful look. "Just like Sam Seasons could, and Chimera Jones. Heroes, not murderers. You remember Sam Seasons, don't you? Hazzard's shoe leather in that series. I was a kid when that series ran. I liked your character so much I hoped then they'd create a whole new series just around you."

"You son of a bitch," Rhodes said softly. "What are you trying to do?"

"Remind you of what you once were, just as I did last night."

"I don't want to be reminded of it! That's dead, and gone, and none of it matters anymore! Nobody cares, and I don't either!"

"I guess you don't," I agreed. "You let yourself die, Rhodes. You've been miscast in your next picture. *You* ought to be the 'thankful corpse.'"

Rhodes gripped Kimberly's shoulder and she winced with pain. "Stand at the top of those stairs! Now!"

I moved back a step, still facing him. "What's it to be this time, Rhodes? A double suicide? The cops won't buy it."

"No, they won't! I'm going to simulate a break-in by a gang, who kill you, rape and murder her, and trash the house. Mindless mayhem, such as this city is accustomed to. Not so *clumsy*, eh?" Rhodes cocked the hammer of the Mauser and aimed straight for my heart. Kimberly began to move, and Rhodes shoved her down to her knees roughly. His face had sagged, but his body hadn't.

He fired, twice. One slug sliced me on the left side and passed through, but the second nailed me in the chest and punched me backwards. It also knocked the wind out of me. I felt myself passing out as I fell and my hands swatted air for something to grasp. It was a long moment and I actually found time to consider what I would think about in my last conscious moments.

Then my rear hit the corner of a step, then my back, and the nape of my neck. My head bounced off the wood of a step. The pain made me fully conscious again and I felt my body slide head-first down the remaining steps and stop when my head cracked against cold concrete. My mouth was open in surprise, and so were my eyes.

I kept them open. I could feel my heart racing and the pain swelling in five different parts of my body. I stared straight up at a light bulb that dangled over the foot of the steps. It hurt my eyes, but I stared. On the periphery of my vision I saw two blurs above me.

"Take a last look at your hero, Kimberly, take a last look at him!"

"Chess!"

Rhodes yanked her away. "Come on, let's get this over with!" I heard fabric tear, then a hard slap. "Upstairs, Saint Kimberly! That's it! Struggle! Fight, try to claw me!" I heard another, stronger slap, and then their steps on the hallway rug as Rhodes manhandled her to the stairs. "It's got to look *real*, you see."

I didn't hear what else he said. My mind stumbled erratically: from pain, to Rhodes, to Kimberly, to dread. Rolling onto my side, I slid the rest of the way onto the cement floor. My wrist watch dug into the first wound, and I cried out.

I knew he'd heard me. The thumping racket and voices on the staircase above stopped. I heard a small crack, metal striking bone. Running steps on the hallway carpet.

I pulled myself out of the direct line of fire. There was a rack of garden tools a few feet away. I took a spade. He started down the stairs. His Mauser was aimed down as I came around the bottom of the stairs and he fired. I swung the spade up, held it far in front of me like a bayoneted rifle as if I could bat away the slugs. His first shot went over my head. He dropped the gun an inch and fired again. The spade flew from my hands with a loud, flat "ping" that stung the bones of my wrists. My foot slipped on the spade handle, and then I was on my knees, three steps from Rhodes's shoes.

He knew what I was going to do and moved the gun to fire into my face. I wrapped my arms around his legs and dug my face into them. There was an explosion and I felt a canal of red pain plow down my back. I felt him bend down and press the muzzle of the gun into my back. I let go of the legs, grabbed his shoulders and yanked. His weight shifted. He could have dropped the gun and grabbed the railing. But he was too intent on killing me. His weight slammed my back as he somersaulted past.

He yelled, hit the basement wall, then the floor. I twisted, expecting another shot. He was on his back, arms and legs flung out, his head on the cement at my feet. A sound like "Awh" erupted from his mouth and didn't stop. I stood up, spotted the Mauser a few feet away. As I retrieved it, I watched Rhodes. He followed me with his eyes. He was still making that sound. There was a plea in his eyes for me to do something. I nudged his ribs with the toe of my shoe.

He screamed and fainted.

His head was canted to one side, but I wasn't interested in that. It was his shoe. Embedded in the rubber sole, bits of blue glass sparkled, tiny as grains of sand.

I limped up the steps, looked down when I realized I'd reached the landing. The trail of blood I saw was my own. I shut the basement door and turned the lock latch.

Rhodes's cap and sunglasses and some buttons from his raincoat were scattered in the hallway. Kimberly lay on the steps half way up to the second floor. Most of her blouse had been torn off. A trickle of blood came from one corner of her mouth, and one side of her face was turning black and blue. I reached down and felt the back of her head, and located a small bruise just above the hairline. But she was breathing.

I took off my jacket and draped it over her. Things slipped from the jacket pockets: a pen, my brass card case, my nickel cigarette case. The pen, a gold Cross refillable, was bent and had leaked ink all over my shirt. The card case had a shadow of a dent in it. And the cigarette case had stopped Rhodes's second slug, which had spent its energy blasting a hole into the lid. I nudged it with my shoe and heard the slug rattle inside. For some reason, I thought that was amusing.

I leaned back and rested my head on Kimberly's arm.

Epilogue

I'd started the case with an emotional certainty. Rhodes ended it with a factual one. I could live with the knowledge I'd gained. Rhodes probably could never have lived with his. That was the only doubt he'd left me room to grant him.

A surgeon mended the long peroneal muscle of my left leg and marveled afterward at the idea that I'd been able to move with a slug in it. I had a long scar on my back from the slug that had plowed diagonally across the skin. And the winging Rhodes gave me with the first shot on the left side of my chest just added another scar to the two already there from past cases. Four out of six of his shots had hit me. I'd pushed the odds and should have been dead. While I was in the hospital, I was asked by curious doctors and nurses what had saved me. I would pull out my mangled cigarette case and rattle the slug that was still inside. I'd inherited the case from my father; it was over half a century old. I added it to my collection of souvenirs of past paradoxes.

When Navarro had reached the house after the local police, he found Kimberly holding my head in her lap, bathing my brow with a cold, wet sponge. I'd passed out and didn't regain consciousness until a nurse woke me so I could sign some papers for an operation. Then she put me to sleep again.

Kimberly came to my room every day while I recovered. We talked, played some cards, and talked more. She recovered, too, rediscovering a self I'd never met.

One day, watching the rain fall outside my hospital room window, she said, "Chess, I'd thought I'd met evil men before, in the business, men so low and predatory and vile that I couldn't imagine how they could live with themselves from day to day. But—it was so much more intense in Rhodes . . . that night. He didn't touch you, so *you* couldn't feel it. Can you explain him?"

After a moment of reflection, I said, "He was once a moral man. He portrayed moral men, and was good at it. But his own character, the one that animated Chimera Jones and Sam Seasons, had never been tested in the world beyond the camera. When he had to emulate in real life what his fictitious characters were on screen, he folded. Victory in real life wasn't a script-written guarantee. He soured." I paused. "That's my diagnosis. You'd have to ask him, or Player, but you'd never get a straight answer. I didn't. All they gave me were excuses for their actions."

Kimberly studied me. "You were a kind of mirror to him, Chess. You're what he'd given up being. You were a reproach."

And sooner or later, he'd have come after me. He'd have wanted to erase me from his memory—from reality.

When she came back the next day and sat on the bed beside me, I asked, "Will you marry me?"

She smiled. "It would be a difficult and stormy marriage, Chess."

I nodded in agreement. "But not for *us*."

Professor Robert Downey called her at home after the story hit the papers. The thing he'd remembered and wanted to tell me was that he'd seen Munro and Rhodes together in a Queens Village restaurant one evening after school. "We didn't speak or anything," he'd told Kimberly. "But I recall knowing who it was Forbes was with and that he was a star, and I even remarked to my wife how much his looks had deteriorated. Then a while ago I saw his picture in the paper about a new movie he's supposed to be in."

Elliott Rhodes's back was not broken but was dislocated and damaged at several points. He also had a shattered pelvis, several fractured ribs, and a mild concussion. When he was able to speak, he said nothing. Nevertheless, he was arraigned on two charges of first-degree murder, Munro's and Cynthia Vogel's. The glass on the bottom of his shoes matched that found in the closet and halls at Ploughsmith College. I'd picked out a fancy Belgian vase and there was nothing else like it in the city.

Patrick Player, I learned from Kimberly and the papers, hired a notoriously successful criminal defense lawyer to represent his friend and future costar. Of course, the D.A.'s staff already had my story and Navarro's file to back it up. When the notorious attorney reported back to Player about his preliminary meeting with the D.A., Player abruptly withdrew his help and dropped Rhodes from the cast of *The Thankful Corpse*. The papers had a field day with the defection, especially Ellen Romero, who forgave me for not giving her the scoop I'd promised.

Elliott Rhodes never did go to trial. One night, three weeks after I'd flung him down the steps, he moved in his sleep, broke some healing vertebrae, hemorrhaged, and went into a coma. He died a week later. I didn't feel cheated of justice, and neither did Kimberly. Everyone knew why he was in that hospital bed, and who had put him there.

Patrick Player went ahead with production of *The Thankful Corpse*, replacing Rhodes with Vinnie Vargo, an actor whose slapstick detective series was cancelled after half a season on television. The picture flopped when it was released, and speculation in Hollywood trade publications was that it flopped for reasons other than because it was a stinker. There was a falling out between Player's Autumn Harvest Productions and Twin Dolphins over future projects—now that Rhodes was gone—and a week before Autumn Harvest was scheduled to be listed on the New York Stock Exchange, a spokesman for Player sullenly declared it bankrupt at a brief press conference.

Kimberly made me stay in the hospital long enough so that I could move around on a crutch. "I couldn't bear to see you in a wheelchair," she'd explained to me one day after she returned from feeding Walker in my apartment. And a week after I'd discarded the crutch, we were quietly married in a private ceremony in Connecticut. Navarro, my best man, was afraid to kiss the bride. I wasn't. Elaine Card was stricken with selective amnesia, once news of our marriage got out, and flooded us with social invitations, which we never answered. But she didn't once try to call on us. She remembered.

Kimberly didn't need to announce her plans to venture back into pictures. By the time we returned from our honeymoon in Europe there were six studio offers waiting in her agent's office, including one from Twin Dolphins. It somewhat thick-headedly tendered the lead in a comedy called *Maximum Strength*, in which she was to portray a woman executive rising to the top of a detergent-manufacturing firm.

We were ready for them. We'd discussed Twin Dolphins in Europe, and had decided what to do about the Munro screen credit, and about the unwanted checks. She had her attorney, John Tigrini, write executive producers Sproule and Grunnian a letter informing them that if the studio did not remove J. Forbes Munro's name from the credits of *Falling Bodies*, she would start litigation against the studio, and use the royalty checks sent to her and to Munro's estate to pay for the suit. She also sent a personal letter that curtly advised the producers not to ever again offer her a role in any of their productions.

My job was to get Ellen Romero to mention the bogus Munro credit in her column. I filled her in on my talk with Player at Soundview, the actor's earlier association with Munro, and even gave her a copy of Munro's original script, *The Stars*

Within, and a video cassette of *Falling Bodies,* which she'd never seen, so that she could make a first-hand judgment.

Which she did. In a three-part series in her *Chronicle* column, she related several anecdotes about the less glamorous aspects of Hollywood, such as the power of its unions, its low esteem for the public and the country, and how great, good, and bad scripts were put through its rewrite grinders.

"Apparently Mr. Player's sense of justice is based on the vendetta code of a gang of juvenile delinquents," she wrote at the end of a scathing synopsis of the actor's film career. "Mr. Munro gave the actor a rotten review, and the actor retaliated by crediting the historian with a rotten movie. The original script had the makings of a great film, and Mr. Player was once a great actor. But it is obvious that he had grown weary of greatness, his own and others'."

Other papers ran their own versions of Romero's column, even some of the Hollywood trade rags. A month after the column ran, Kimberly's attorney received a letter from the legal department of Twin Dolphins, which informed him that all copies of *Falling Bodies* were being recalled so that the credit could be amended to read, "From a screenplay by J. Forbes Munro, adapted by Patrick Player."

Kimberly looked up at me from across the table at Paulette's, where we had gone to talk about Twin Dolphins' concession. "I'm satisfied," she said.

I nodded. "So am I."

Twin Dolphins never again offered her a role. The checks stopped coming to Munro's estate, but Kimberly still gets her own. She tears them up without a thought, with all the other junk mail.

Excelsior Films, which showcased her in *Savoy 9000* and *Fraction of Fear,* made her two offers with a tandem shooting schedule. One picture was called *Hypatia,* in which she would have the title role of a beautiful scholar murdered on the steps of the Alexandria Library, betrayed to a mob of religious zealots by a lover who could not decide between heaven on earth and heaven after earth. The other was *Uncommon Cause,* in which she would portray the daughter of an Italian resistance fighter who is betrayed to the Nazis by the abbot of a monastery. The abbot is now a Papal candidate. The daughter, who learns how and why her father died, is determined to scuttle the aging cardinal's candidacy. Opposing her are the cardinal and forces that want to preserve his image as saint and war hero.

I read the scripts she would work with. I was excited about them, but something was missing. When I realized what it was, I looked up from my reading one evening and asked, "And when are they going to find you a hero?"

She glanced up from the piano where she was practicing Granados's "Orientale," and smiled at me. "When *you* learn how to act," she teased. Then she added, without missing a note on the keyboard, "They'll find me a hero when they look for one. And if they find one, they'll have to give him a good enough reason to come out, and then not to be afraid of him when he does."

Kimberly played on. I leaned back in my reading chair with the newly published collection of essays by J. Forbes Munro, *Essays on the Art of Biography.* I leafed through the pages to the paragraph that had prompted my question:

". . . Why do I concentrate on individual lives instead of on the 'larger picture'? Because the larger picture is already there; it is the raw material of history. Men will act in the circumstances of their knowledge. If they did not, then no history would be possible. And some men will act in so extraordinary a way that they will define the soul of their time, and impress their era with the stamp or seal of their own characters. . . . So these men give meaning to the 'larger picture' they happen to be in."

I closed the book and looked up to study my reflection in the window and evening skyline beyond. I was not afraid of what I saw.

Photo: Cathy Grosfils

About the Author

Edward Cline is the author of several detective novels in addition to his popular historical series *Sparrowhawk*, set in the period leading up to the American Revolution. Another Chess Hanrahan mystery, *With Distinction*, is scheduled for publication by Perfect Crime Books in 2011. New editions of the Sparrowhawk novels are due from Patrick Henry Press. Mr. Cline's nonfiction has appeared in *The Wall Street Journal* and other publications. He lives in Williamsburg, Virginia.

If you enjoyed this book, look for these other Chess Hanrahan mysteries by Edward Cline published by PERFECT CRIME BOOKS.

PRESENCE OF MIND
186 pages. $14.95. ISBN: 978-0-9825157-0-9

Chess Hanrahan, "a thinking man's Mike Hammer", takes on Russian thugs *and* a cabal of American social scientists.
"A fine new private eye series." (James Reasoner)

FIRST PRIZE
198 pages. $13.95. ISBN: 978-0-9825157-7-8

A brilliant young writer disappears after winning a major literary award. Chess Hanrahan finds more than murder in this challenging intellectual mystery,
"Exceptionally strong . . . A striking tale." (Allen J. Hubin, *The Armchair Detective*)

These titles are available at book stores, at Amazon and other on-line retailers, and at www.PerfectCrimeBooks.com.